D0961748

Withdrawn

The Best-Laid Plans of
Jonah Twist

The
Best-Laid Plans
of
Jonah Twist

by Natalie Honeycutt

Simon & Schuster Books for Young Readers

SIMON & SCHUSTER BOOKS FOR YOUNG READERS
An imprint of Simon & Schuster Children's Publishing Division
1230 Avenue of the Americas
New York, New York 10020
Simon & Schuster Books for Young Readers is a trademark of Simon & Schuster
Printed and bound in the United States of America
20 19 18 17 16 15 14 13 12

The text of this book is set in 12 pt. Caledonia.

Library of Congress Cataloging-in-Publication Data

Honeycutt, Natalie.
The best-laid plans of Jonah Twist / by Natalie Honeycutt.   p.   cm.
Summary: Busy third grader Jonah Twist must endure giving a school
report on elephant seals with the bossy Juliet Fisher, while
worrying that his new kitten may have eaten his older brother's
hamster. Sequel to "The All New Jonah Twist."
ISBN 0-02-744850-9
[1. Schools–Fiction.   2. Family life—Fiction.]   I. Title.
PZ7.H7467Be   1988
[Fic]—dc19
88-7288   CIP   AC

For Linda Davenport,
perfection in a friend

The Best-Laid Plans of
Jonah Twist

one

"DON'T forget," Granville called from his front porch.

"I won't," Jonah called back. He wanted to wave to his friend, but his hands were busy. They were holding something wiggly under his sweatshirt. The something wiggly was a kitten.

Right now it was Granville's kitten, one of a litter, but if everything went according to plan, it would soon be Jonah's kitten. The plan was what Granville wanted Jonah not to forget. And the plan, like the kitten, was Granville's.

Jonah Twist wasn't good at plans. He could make a plan, but usually it worked badly. Like the time he had meant to get Granville in trouble, and had ended up in trouble himself. Or Jonah would make a plan and then forget it, which seemed to him worse than no plan at all. But Jonah had hopes that this one would work, because Granville Jones was good at plans.

Granville was Jonah's best friend. He was also

the smallest, fastest, and smartest kid in their third-grade class at Mills Elementary School in Westmont, California. And he was nothing at all like Jonah Twist.

He started the plan by asking Jonah a lot of questions. "When is your mother in a good mood?" Granville asked.

Jonah thought hard. "Saturdays and Sundays," he said at last. His mother didn't go to work on those days, and even though she worked at home she seemed happier. "Except for Sunday evenings," Jonah added. "On Sunday evenings she gets crabby about whether everything is ready for Monday morning." Jonah's mother was a planner, too.

"Is Todd home on Saturdays and Sundays?" Granville asked. Todd was Jonah's older brother.

"Yes," Jonah said. "Except for Saturday mornings when he practices with the cross-country team."

"Then you'll have to do it on Saturday in the morning," Granville said. "Todd could mess up everything for you."

Jonah knew that this was true. And the plan was one that Todd would want to mess up. "Todd thinks that a cat would be dangerous for his hamster," Jonah said.

"No sweat," Granville said. "If he tells that to your mother, you point out that this is a *kitten*, not a cat."

"Oh!" Jonah said. Granville was really good at this stuff.

"Can you get a shoe box?" Granville asked.

"Well, yes," Jonah said, "but I thought I would just carry the kitten in my hands. She likes it when I hold her."

"For a litter box," Granville said. "The shoe box is for litter until you can get a real litter box. Your mother will think of a litter box. Mine did."

"Oh," Jonah said again.

"And money," Granville said. "Do you have any money?"

"Nearly seven dollars," Jonah said. He usually saved his money in case there was something he really wanted.

"Good. Because you'll have to tell your mother you will buy the food yourself. She may even make you. It depends on how tough your mother is."

"Pretty tough," Jonah mumbled. He didn't like to think about it.

"Then you may need to buy a bag of kitten food the first time. But don't worry, your mother will probably buy it after that."

"If I get to keep the kitten at all," Jonah said. "I'm not so sure this will work."

"It'll work," Granville said. "You'll see."

Jonah repeated that to himself as he walked down the sidewalk toward home. The bulge under his sweatshirt had ceased to wiggle and had started to purr. He could feel the kitten with his hands.

Jonah cut across Mr. Rosetti's yard and turned onto Sonora Street. He wanted to ring Mr. Rosetti's doorbell and show him the kitten. But then he might forget some of the details of the plan. He continued on down Sonora Street toward home.

Jonah stopped at the front walk to his house and thought about what to say first. "Mom, look at this!" he would say. "Isn't it cute?" Granville had said to sound enthusiastic.

Inside, Jonah pushed the front door closed with his foot and walked through the living room looking for his mother. He walked through the dining room and into the kitchen. Then he walked through the kitchen to the laundry room. His mother was in there.

"Jonah, look at this!" his mother said. "Isn't it awful?" She held up Jonah's 49er's T-shirt. It was covered with flesh-colored spots. "And look at

4

this," she said. She held up Jonah's blue pajama bottoms.

They were also covered with flesh-colored spots.

Mrs. Twist reached into the washer and pulled out Jonah's plaid sheet. It had spots as well.

"Silly Putty!" his mother exclaimed. "You must have left your Silly Putty in a pocket. Or maybe you left it in your bed and I didn't see it. But now there is Silly Putty on every single thing in this load of laundry!" She was almost yelling.

Jonah gulped.

"I don't know what I'm going to do with you," she went on. "I have asked you time and again to be careful where you leave things."

"I forgot," Jonah said softly.

"Well, you have to start remembering, Jonah. Responsible people don't forget." She dropped the laundry back into the machine and pushed in the knob. Then she poured in some soap. It wasn't laundry soap. It was the stuff she used on the kitchen floor.

"I hope this works," she said, and slammed down the lid to the washer. The noise made the kitten start, and Jonah clutched it more firmly against his stomach.

Jonah followed his mother as she went into the kitchen. He didn't know what to say to her about the Silly Putty. He was afraid to say anything, really, in case she started to yell. When she began to rummage in the refrigerator, Jonah walked quietly past her and into the living room. He sat on the couch to think.

There wasn't anything in Granville's plan about Silly Putty. Jonah was sure of that. So what should he do now? Should he take the kitten back to Granville's house? Should he hide it in his room until later?

While he was thinking, Jonah's mother came into the room. She slumped into the overstuffed yellow chair and took a sip from a can of soda. The kitten began to squirm under Jonah's sweatshirt.

"I'm not very happy with you right now," his mother announced.

"I know," Jonah said. Back to Granville's, he said to himself. He stood up and headed toward the door.

"Jonah," his mother said, "where are you going?"

"Well . . ." Jonah said.

"And why are you holding your stomach? Jonah, are you ill?"

"No," Jonah said. "Not exactly."

"Well, what . . ."

At that moment the kitten wriggled free of Jonah's grasp and tumbled out the bottom of his sweatshirt. It landed with a soft plop on the carpet.

"Uh-oh," Jonah said.

The kitten shook its head, then sat blinking at its surroundings.

"Oh, no," Mrs. Twist said.

"Mom, look at this," Jonah said in a flat, dull voice. "Isn't it cute?"

"Jonah . . ." his mother began. There was a warning in the way she said it.

"It's Granville's," Jonah said. Was he supposed to say that? He couldn't remember.

"Then I think you'd better take it back to Granville," Mrs. Twist said.

The plan, the plan. What was he supposed to do if his mother said to take it back? Oh, yes . . . "I can't. I told Granville I'd keep it overnight. To help out."

He was careful not to say who the help was for.

"Oh, Jonah," his mother said. "You should have checked first."

"I'm checking now," Jonah ventured.

"Well . . ." The kitten had found its way across the room and was batting at motes of dust in the sunlight. Mrs. Twist watched it for a minute.

Then she cocked her head. Then she smiled. "I suppose one night wouldn't hurt."

"Yea!" Jonah exclaimed. *Yea* wasn't in the plan, but he couldn't help saying it.

Jonah picked up the kitten and walked over to his mother. "I think it looks a little like the marmots we see when we go camping with Dad in the Sierra," he said. "It's the colors. Mostly orangish brown with some white and black."

"I would have called it a calico," his mother said. "But I see what you mean." She reached out and stroked the kitten on its head.

"Here, you can hold it," Jonah said, putting the kitten on his mother's lap. This was the most important part of the plan. Granville said that if Jonah's mother held the kitten awhile, she would "bond" with it. Then she would *want* Jonah to keep the kitten. Granville said that was why mothers kept ugly babies, because they held them and bonded.

"It *is* awfully cute," his mother said.

That Granville Jones was a genius!

"It's a girl," Jonah said. "I was thinking . . ."

At that moment, Todd slammed through the front door. He dropped his gym bag on the floor and limped to the couch where he sprawled, one leg on the couch, one foot on the floor.

"That Randy McKnight," he said. "He's such a

dork! He could have ruined my whole running career."

"Todd, what happened?" Mrs. Twist sounded alarmed.

"McKnight doesn't even know how to pass," Todd said. "I don't know why they even let him on the cross-country team. Just because he has long legs, I guess. But we couldn't have been more than fifty yards out of the starting line when all of a sudden he puts on the steam, which was *way* too early anyhow, and tries to pass me. Instead he crashes into me and I wrench my ankle."

"Oh, Todd," Mrs. Twist said. "Do you need to see a doctor?"

"Naw. Coach put some ice on it and said I should rest it for a couple of days. But he says it's okay. Still . . ." Todd paused. "What's *that*?" He pointed at the kitten.

"A kitten," Mrs. Twist said. "Isn't it dear?" She lifted it to her face and nuzzled it.

"I can see it's a kitten," Todd said. "But what's it doing here?"

"Jonah is taking care of it for Granville," Mrs. Twist said. She set the kitten on the floor.

"Ha!" Todd said. "Taking care of it, my eye. I bet he wants to keep it."

Jonah wanted to protest, but he couldn't think

of the right words. If he said no, he'd have to take the kitten back. And if he said yes, his mother might catch on. Todd could really mess things up!

The kitten began to chase its tail. It raced in circles and tumbled head over heels. Then it leapt straight up in the air and landed with its feet splayed. Jonah laughed. His mother laughed. Todd was silent.

"I expect Jonah does want to keep it," Mrs. Twist said.

"Well, you're not going to let him, are you?" Todd demanded.

"I'm not sure," she said. "I'm thinking about it."

"Really?" Jonah said. Wow!

"Mom!" Todd said. "You can't let him keep it. You said Jonah has to be responsible to have a pet. And he's nowhere *near* being responsible. If you ask me, he never will be, either."

Mrs. Twist looked hard at Todd. "I didn't ask you, Todd," she said in an even voice. "And what's more, I don't plan to ask you."

Jonah felt confused. Did this mean he would get to keep the kitten? Or did it only mean that Todd didn't get to decide? None of this stuff was in Granville's plan.

"I'll be responsible," Jonah said. "I clear my dishes almost every time now, and the Silly Putty was an accident. I have the shoe box and the money. And I wouldn't leave a kitten in my pocket." Jonah stopped. He hadn't meant to remind his mother about the Silly Putty.

"Jonah," his mother said. "I know you want to be responsible. I think we should talk about the Silly Putty another time, don't you?"

"What Silly Putty?" Todd asked.

"The Silly Putty in my pocket that ruined the wash," Jonah muttered.

"Aha!" Todd said. "See?"

"Never mind," Mrs. Twist said. "Jonah also got a very good report card from Mrs. Lacey two days ago, if you remember."

Jonah certainly remembered. Mrs. Lacey had written, "Jonah tries very hard. He does his best." It was the best report card Jonah had gotten in his entire life.

"But I don't think you'll want to keep a kitten in a shoe box," his mother went on. "Kittens need to run around."

"I know that," Jonah said. The kitten was running around right now. He explained about the litter, and that the money was for buying the food.

"I can tell you've given this a lot of thought," his mother said.

Somebody did, Jonah said to himself.

"Did you happen to think about a name, too?" she asked.

"Yeah," Jonah said. "I thought we could name her Einstein. In case she turns out to be smart."

"That's dumb," Todd said.

"Maybe *Mrs.* Einstein would suit her better," Mrs. Twist said. "She'd probably appreciate having a girl's name."

"That's what I meant," Jonah said. "Mrs. Einstein."

"Why don't you just call her Killer?" Todd said. "Cats kill hamsters, you know. They scare them to death. Doesn't anyone here care what happens to Woz?" Woz was Todd's hamster.

"No sweat," Jonah said confidently. "This is a kitten, not a cat!" Then he turned to his mother. He should ask her now. He was sure this was the moment.

"Mom," Jonah said, "can I keep this kitten? I'll take good care of her, and I'll even pay for her food. So can I?"

"May I," Mrs. Twist corrected. "And yes, you may keep Mrs. Einstein."

"Yea!" Jonah hollered.

"Swell," Todd said.

Mrs. Twist drained the last of her can of soda and stood up. She picked up Mrs. Einstein and stroked her under the chin. "And don't worry about paying for the food, Jonah," she said. "I've always bought Woz's food. I think I can buy the food for Mrs. Einstein."

"I don't think you'll have to worry about Woz's food much longer," Todd said as he limped from the room. "Dead hamsters don't eat much."

two

On Monday morning things started going wrong. First thing, just after the Pledge of Allegiance, Mrs. Lacey let people share. Granville had a new combat helmet, and he shared about that. Then some other kids shared. But time ran out before Jonah could share about Mrs. Einstein.

Next, Mrs. Lacey started talking about habitat studies. "We're going to start on Part Two of our habitat studies," she said. "For this part, we will observe animals in their natural environments. And this time, we're going to work in teams."

Kids began to ask questions. Some raised their hands, and some didn't bother.

"Can we observe insects?" Sarah asked.

"Yes," Mrs. Lacey said.

"Can we observe our own pets?" Greg asked.

"Yes, you may observe your own pets," she said. "You may observe any living creature you like, so long as it doesn't live in a cage. A cage is not a very natural environment."

That leaves out Woz, Jonah thought.

Granville leaned over from his seat next to Jonah's and whispered, "Hey, you can observe Mrs. Einstein!"

"Yeah," Jonah said. That would be easy. Jonah liked to watch Mrs. Einstein.

Mrs. Lacey went on to explain about working in teams. There should be three people on a team. And it might be a good idea to choose teammates who lived nearby, as some of the observations would be homework. She gave the class five minutes to choose teams while she wrote on the chalkboard.

Jonah thought she should have plugged her ears; everyone started talking at once, and kids got out of their seats and started grabbing one another.

Granville slung an arm over Jonah's shoulder. "Partners!" he said.

"Partners!" Jonah agreed.

"If we have to draw pictures, you can do the drawing," Granville said. "That's one of the things you're good at."

That was true. And besides, Jonah liked to draw. "And you can do the writing," Jonah said. "That's one of the things I'm *not* good at. Besides, I hate it."

"You only hate it because it's hard for you,"

Granville said. "But I don't mind." He stood on tiptoes and began scanning the room.

"We'd better hurry and get someone else," he said.

"How about Robbie?" Jonah still thought of Robbie as one of his best friends, even though they hadn't played together all year.

"Sure. But you'd better go get him quick," Granville said. "Everyone is getting picked."

Jonah shoved back his chair and made his way across the noisy room to Robbie. Robbie was talking to Greg and Kevin, so Jonah had to wait to talk to him. It was rude to interrupt.

Finally Jonah's moment came. "Want to work with me and Granville?" he asked.

"Sorry," Robbie said. "I'm working with these guys."

Jonah made his way back to his seat. Just as he was explaining to Granville that Robbie had already been chosen, Mrs. Lacey called the class to order.

"Is there anyone who isn't on a team?" she asked.

Jonah watched to see who put a hand up. He didn't want to get stuck with a leftover.

No hands went up.

"Whew!" Jonah said.

"Very well," Mrs. Lacey said. "Are there any teams with only two people on them?"

Jonah and Granville raised their hands. So did Sara and Mindy.

"Uh-oh," Jonah said.

"That's just right," said Mrs. Lacey. "We have a couple of people absent today: Elizabeth Chin and Juliet Fisher. One for each team."

Granville turned to Jonah. "Elizabeth," he said.

"Right," said Jonah.

Granville shot his hand into the air.

"We'll take Elizabeth!" Sara called out.

"Hey, no fair!" Granville protested.

Jonah groaned and slumped down in his seat. Juliet Fisher was his least favorite person in the whole class. Possibly the entire world.

"Well," Mrs. Lacey said, "it does make more sense for Juliet to work with Granville and Jonah. She lives in their neighborhood. Elizabeth will work with Sara and Mindy."

Jonah wondered whether Mrs. Lacey would believe him if he said that Juliet had moved. He looked helplessly at Granville.

"That's the last time I'm ever raising my hand in this class," Granville said. "From now on I call out, just like the rest of the goons."

Jonah hardly heard the rest of Mrs. Lacey's instructions about the habitat observations. All he could think about was how lousy it would be to work with Juliet. The Announcer. The Know-It-All. The Boss of the World. It took him until lunchtime, when he found carrot sticks in his lunch, to forget about her. Carrot sticks were worse than Juliet. But just barely.

During the afternoon, Jonah had trouble keeping his mind on his work. He kept thinking about Mrs. Einstein. This was her first day home alone, and Jonah hoped she wasn't lonely. He could see her in his mind, playing with the toy mouse that his mother had bought when she got the cat food. Mrs. Einstein swatted the mouse with her paw. Then she picked it up by the tail and, with her head held high, pranced across the living room. Then she climbed on the couch, dragging the mouse with her. Jonah hoped that if Mrs. Einstein got lonely she would remember about the mouse.

After school, Granville set his lunch box on the ground near his feet while he adjusted the chin strap on his new helmet.

Jonah thought that the helmet made Granville look more awesome than ever. It was an army surplus helmet, covered in camouflage cloth. Since Jonah and Granville had become friends,

Jonah often forgot that Granville was the littlest person in the whole third grade. Sometimes, like now, Granville seemed like a giant.

"I think Mrs. Lacey must have lost her mind over the weekend," Granville said. He gave his helmet a slap.

"Mrs. Lacey never lets anyone wear a hat in school," Jonah said. "Remember when Kenny Ota came back from Texas in that cowboy hat? Mrs. Lacey made him take it off, too."

"Not that, dummy." Granville picked up his lunch box. "Making us work with Juliet. I call *that* losing your mind."

"Oh, yeah," Jonah said. He had forgotten about Juliet. In fact, he wanted to forget about her for good.

"Come on," Granville said. "I'll race you home."

This was the same thing Granville said almost every day. Usually Jonah agreed to race. And always Granville won.

Jonah caught up with Granville on his front porch. Granville's helmet was off, and he was leaning against the rail eating a cookie.

"I've figured out what to do about Juliet," he said. Crumbs sprayed from his mouth as he spoke.

Jonah dropped his lunch box on the steps.

"The only thing that would help is if she moved. And I don't think that's going to happen."

"No, we'll choose a really yucky animal to observe. Then she'll quit!"

Jonah thought this over. "Hmmmm," he said. "It might work."

"Sure it will," Granville said.

"Yeah, but what animal?" Jonah asked. "A crocodile?" That might work. Hardly anybody could stand crocodiles.

"Well, I was thinking of a boa constrictor. But a crocodile would do it. Good thinking, Jonah!" Granville thumped Jonah on the back.

Jonah beamed. Usually Granville had the good ideas. It was nice to have one of his own. It must come from being around Mrs. Einstein, he thought.

"But do you really think she'd quit?" Jonah asked. "Mrs. Lacey might not let her."

"But you know Juliet," Granville said. "She's stubborn. And she knows how to make a fuss. I bet Mrs. Lacey would have to let her quit if she wants to."

"*If* she wants to," Jonah said.

"She'll want to," Granville said. "That's our job—to make sure she wants to." He tossed the rest of the cookie in his mouth and added, "By the time we're done with her, she may quit school!"

"YEA!" Jonah hollered. He could already imagine Juliet cleaning out her desk. Granville was brilliant! What would Jonah do without him? First the kitten, and now getting rid of Juliet for good.

"I've got to go," Jonah said. "I want to take Mrs. Einstein and show her to Mr. Rosetti."

"Think crocodiles!" Granville called as Jonah ran down the walk.

"I'm thinking!" Jonah called back.

Jonah got the key from the flowerpot beside the house and let himself in the front door. He set his binder on the stairs leading to the second story and took his lunch box to the kitchen. Then he opened the lunch box, took out his Thermos, and rinsed it out under the kitchen faucet.

There. That would make his mother happy. She would see she had been right in thinking he was responsible enough to have a pet.

"Mrs. Einstein," Jonah called. "Here kitty, Mrs. Einstein." He walked through the downstairs rooms, looking under furniture, calling for the kitten. Her toy mouse lay on the living room couch. But Mrs. Einstein was nowhere to be seen.

Jonah picked up his binder and went upstairs. He looked in his room for Mrs. Einstein. Then he walked down the hall to his mother's room. The door was closed, but he looked in there anyway. Still no Mrs. Einstein.

Then Jonah went back past his room to Todd's. The door to Todd's room was cracked open a few inches. "Uh-oh," Jonah said. He pushed open the door and went in.

There was Mrs. Einstein. She was curled up, asleep, on Todd's desk. Or, rather, on top of Woz's cage, which was on Todd's desk. Woz was nowhere to be seen.

"Oh, Mrs. Einstein!" Jonah said. Had she eaten Woz? He picked up the kitten and looked at her tummy. It was bulgy, but not bulgy enough to account for an entire hamster.

The kitten blinked and looked at Jonah. She opened her mouth and mewed. Jonah smiled. He liked it when he could see in the kitten's mouth. It was so pink and new looking. Jonah decided Mrs. Einstein was happy to see him. He put her down and gave Woz's cage a little shake.

"Woz?" he said.

The bottom of the cage was covered with cedar shavings, and it was hard to tell if Woz was in there or not. Jonah took a pencil and probed gently at the shavings through the bars of the cage. The pencil hit something solid, and Woz emerged, looking bleary.

"Go back to sleep," Jonah said. He took Mrs. Einstein and left Todd's room, closing the door firmly behind him.

Downstairs, Jonah watched Mrs. Einstein eat some food. Then he popped the kitten into his sweatshirt. "We're going to see someone," he said. "His name is Mr. Rosetti."

When Jonah thought about friends, he always thought of Mr. Rosetti. Most kids, Jonah knew, would think of Mr. Rosetti as an old man instead of a friend. And he certainly was old. Jonah didn't know exactly how old Mr. Rosetti was, but old enough to have white hair and lots of wrinkles. And brown spots on his hands.

To Jonah, though, he had always been a friend—ever since the day he had invited Jonah to ride his bike across his front lawn. And at Halloween, just past, Jonah'd had the biggest pumpkin in the neighborhood, thanks to Mr. Rosetti's garden.

Jonah pushed Mr. Rosetti's doorbell and stood waiting. The kitten squirmed under his sweatshirt.

"Just a minute," he said to Mrs. Einstein.

"Sometimes Mr. Rosetti takes a long time."

In a minute he pushed the doorbell again. Mr. Rosetti was taking a longer time than usual.

The kitten squirmed some more. "Let's go around back," Jonah said. "Sometimes Mr. Rosetti works in his garden."

Jonah walked down the steps, then up the driveway to Mr. Rosetti's backyard. He pulled the rope that opened the latch to Mr. Rosetti's backyard gate. Then he went in.

Mr. Rosetti wasn't in the backyard. But Jonah could tell that he had been there recently, because his rake and spade were lying on the ground. Mr. Rosetti had often pointed out to Jonah that he always put his tools away when he was done working. He said that taking care of your tools was important.

As he left the yard, Jonah noticed that Mr. Rosetti's garbage cans were standing empty, their lids on the ground. That was the way garbage cans always looked right after the garbage men had come to collect the garbage. They always left the lids on the ground.

There was something odd about seeing the empty cans and the lids, and Jonah had to think hard to figure out what it was. Then he knew. Today was Monday, and the garbage men came on Thursday.

Jonah walked to the front of the house and rang the bell again. But as he waited, he got the idea that Mr. Rosetti wasn't coming to the door. And for a good reason: Mr. Rosetti wasn't home.

That's when Jonah noticed the newspapers. There were four of them scattered around the front porch.

Jonah thought about the newspapers. Then he thought about the garbage cans again. Then he thought about the rake and the spade.

"Guess what?" he said aloud. "Mr. Rosetti is missing!"

three

"WOULD you ask him to stop saying that?" Todd said to Mrs. Twist. "He's driving me crazy."

"But he *is* missing," Jonah said.

"Jonah, we discussed all of this last night," his mother said.

Jonah dropped his spoon into his cereal bowl and slumped back in his chair, arms dangling. Why wouldn't they listen to him? Just because he sometimes made mistakes . . .

"I'll tell you what," Mrs. Twist said. "I know you're very worried about Mr. Rosetti, so if he still hasn't collected his papers by the time you get home from school, let me know."

"And then what?" Jonah asked.

"Then we'll see," she said.

Jonah knew his mother. He knew that often when she said, "we'll see," it was just an excuse to do nothing for a while longer. But Jonah didn't want to do nothing. It seemed to him that Mr. Rosetti was getting more missing every minute, while everyone did nothing.

26

"But the rake," Jonah pressed on. "Mr. Rosetti wouldn't leave his rake out."

"Except he did leave it out," Todd said. "That's obvious. Old people forget things sometimes. He probably went on vacation and just forgot about the rake and the newspapers."

"He wouldn't," Jonah said.

"Todd's right," Mrs. Twist said. "Old people do forget things sometimes."

Young people, too, Jonah thought. He forgot more things than anybody he knew. But he didn't want to remind Todd and his mother of that right now.

"The spade, too," Jonah said. "He left his spade out, too."

"Mom," Todd said, "just tell him to stop talking. He'll stop if you tell him to."

"Jonah," Mrs. Twist said, "I told you . . ."

"I know, I know," Jonah said. " 'We'll see.' " He picked up his cereal bowl and carried it to the kitchen sink. Then he took his lunch box and his binder and went to the front door.

He bent to pet Mrs. Einstein, who had scampered after him. "See you later," he said. He didn't say good-bye to anyone else until the door had closed behind him. And then he said it softly.

As soon as Jonah walked into Room 4B at Mills

Elementary School he spotted Juliet Fisher. She was sitting at her desk doing the same thing she did every morning—tidying her binder.

Juliet already had the neatest binder of anybody in the third grade. But every morning she sat down at her desk while everyone else was still milling about, and opened her binder. Then she began to leaf through it. She paused occasionally to open the rings and move a paper from one place to another. Jonah didn't know exactly why it bothered him to see her do this each morning, but it did.

He sank into his seat next to Granville, dreading social studies. He didn't have to dread it long, because it was the first thing Mrs. Lacey mentioned.

"This morning," she said, "we're going to break into our groups for the habitat study. The first order of business will be for each group to decide what animal it will observe. After that, we will talk about what kinds of things might be important to observe, and how we will record our observations."

She stopped a moment to glance at a piece of paper she held in her hand. "Juliet," she said. "You weren't here when we chose our groups, so I have assigned you to work with Jonah and Granville."

Juliet's head jerked, as if someone had just hit her. "Not them!" she said.

Several kids laughed. Jonah felt confused. Were they laughing at him and Granville, or at Juliet?

"That's okay," Granville said loudly, "we don't want to work with you, either." The laughter was louder this time.

Mrs. Lacey waited quietly until the laughter had died, then said, "I'm sure three such nice people will get along very well."

Granville ducked his head and muttered, just loud enough for Jonah to hear, "That's all she knows."

Jonah shook his head. There was something about the way Mrs. Lacey had spoken that sounded as though she were giving an order.

Chairs scraped noisily across the floor as people rearranged themselves into groups of three. Juliet plunked down into a chair near Jonah and Granville. She folded her arms across her chest and glared.

"Well," Granville said. He nudged Jonah.

"Well," Jonah said uncertainly.

"Guess we have to choose an animal," Granville said.

Juliet sniffed. "It can't be a cat," she said. "I'm allergic."

"We don't want to do a cat, anyway," Granville said.

"No," Jonah agreed.

"Or a dog," Juliet said. "I'm allergic to them, too."

Granville smiled. "No dogs, either," he said. He nudged Jonah again. "Go ahead, tell her."

"Oh," Jonah said. He faltered. "It's just . . . well, we decided it would be fun to do a . . . a crocodile!"

"A crocodile!" Juliet screeched.

"Yes," Jonah said proudly. It was a great idea, he could see that now.

"Forget it," Juliet said. "I'm not doing a yucky crocodile. They're gross. They're disgusting."

"And dangerous!" Granville added.

"That's right," Juliet said. "They're very dangerous. So no crocodiles!"

"But that's what we want to do," Granville said.

"I don't!" Juliet said. She was getting really mad.

Granville turned to Jonah and gave him a wicked grin. "We could vote," he said. "I vote for crocodiles." He stuck his hand in the air.

Jonah thrust his hand up as well. "Me, too," he said.

30

"No fair," Juliet said.

"We voted," Granville said. "It's two against one."

"Then I quit!" Juliet said. She pushed back her chair and marched off to Mrs. Lacey.

Granville clapped Jonah on the back. "See?" he said. "It worked!"

"Yeah," Jonah said. He watched Juliet in disbelief. "I didn't think it would be so easy."

"To tell the truth, neither did I," Granville said. "But ol' Juliet really likes to have things her own way."

In a minute, though, Juliet was back, standing in front of Granville and Jonah.

"I'm back," she announced, and took her seat.

Jonah and Granville exchanged an uneasy look. Neither of them spoke.

"In case you're wondering why I'm back, it's because Mrs. Lacey says you can't do crocodiles."

"Why not?" Jonah and Granville asked.

"Because," Juliet said, "Mrs. Lacey says the only crocodiles in Northern California are in cages, which is not a natural environment." Her voice was heavy with disdain.

"Oh," Granville said.

"We didn't think of that," Jonah mumbled.

They sat silently for a moment, Juliet looking defiant, Jonah and Granville studying their feet.

Something banged around in Jonah's head, trying to get out. An idea. If he could just think what it was . . . "A boa constrictor!" he said. That was it!

"Sorry," Juliet sneered, "that's the same. They're only in cages."

Jonah groaned. He should have thought of that himself. "Rattlesnakes!" he said. "There are plenty of rattlesnakes in Northern California. And most of them aren't in cages. They're under rocks in fields. I even know how to look for them!" Another great idea! He seemed to be full of them these days.

"That's way too dangerous," Juliet said.

"No, it's not," Jonah said. This time he nudged Granville.

Granville stared at Jonah, openmouthed. Jonah could tell Granville was thinking what a great idea rattlesnakes were.

"Excuse us," Granville said to Juliet. "Me and my buddy need to have a conversation." He hauled Jonah by the shirt-sleeve to a private corner of the room.

"You're either very brave or very cuckoo," Granville said.

"Brave," Jonah said proudly.

"Jonah, rattlesnakes have venom. It's poison!"

"I know that," Jonah said.

"And they bite," Granville said.

"Well," Jonah said, "only when they're scared or mad."

"But they get mad or scared when someone finds them!" Granville said.

"Oh," Jonah said. He had forgotten that.

"And since you're the one that knows how to find them, you're the one that will probably get bitten."

"Oh," Jonah said again. He was beginning to feel a lot less brave.

"And you'll die," Granville said flatly.

Jonah took a deep breath. "Too dangerous, huh?" he said.

"Way too dangerous," Granville said. "Not that I like to agree with Juliet."

Jonah sighed. "So what do we do now?"

"I don't know. Maybe we should tell Juliet to think of something."

"What good would that do?" Jonah asked.

"Well, at least we can say no to all of her ideas while we think," Granville said.

Just as if she had read their minds, Juliet was ready with plenty of ideas.

When they returned to their seats, she said, "There's a mockingbird in my backyard. We could observe that."

"Naw, a cat might get it," Granville said.

"Right," Jonah agreed.

"Gophers, then," Juliet said. "The park is full of gophers."

"Too hard to see," Jonah said. He had once spent an entire afternoon waiting beside a gopher hole, so he knew.

"Right," Granville agreed.

"Well, how about seals?" Juliet asked. "There are plenty of them, and they're easy to see. We could take some binoculars and watch the seals on Seal Rock."

Jonah racked his brain. There must be something wrong with seals, though he couldn't think just what. Truthfully, he thought seals were cute.

"Uh . . ." Granville said. He, too, seemed at a loss.

Juliet went on. "There are California sea lions and harbor seals. We could choose. There are even elephant seals, though I hate them. They're so ugly."

Granville didn't miss a beat. "Elephant seals!" he cried.

"We love them!" Jonah said.

Juliet buried her head in her hands. "Oh, no . . ." she moaned.

"Elephant seals are the best!" Granville went on. "We could even watch them have babies. Of course, I've heard they roll on some of the babies and squish them to death."

"Ick!" Juliet said. "That's disgusting!"

That did it. "Let's vote," Granville said. "All for elephant seals . . ."

He stuck his hand in the air.

Jonah promptly did the same.

"No fair!" Juliet said.

"Two against one," Jonah said.

"Then I quit!" Juliet said. Again she stood and marched off to Mrs. Lacey. Jonah and Granville exchanged a victorious look.

But in a minute Juliet was back, a bright red spot on each cheek. "Mrs. Lacey says elephant seals are okay," she announced. Then she flung herself into her seat and glowered at them. "She also said I can't quit."

Jonah was so discouraged at the failure of their plan for getting rid of Juliet that he never even thought of Mr. Rosetti until the middle of spelling. They were working on words that ended with *-ing* like *rocking* and *going*, which reminded Jonah of the word *missing*.

Jonah leaned over to Granville and whispered, "Mr. Rosetti is missing."

"Where did he go?" Granville asked.

"I don't know," Jonah said. "But I don't think he went someplace, I think he vanished. If he had gone someplace, he would have put his rake away first."

Granville looked at Jonah and blinked. He seemed to be thinking. Then he said, "Mr. Rosetti always puts his tools away." Granville would know that. He lived next door to Mr. Rosetti. "If he went somewhere without putting away his tools, he probably went in a big hurry."

"I know," Jonah said.

"So where?" Granville asked. "In a UFO?"

"Those are made up," Jonah said.

"Maybe," Granville said.

"Definitely."

Granville shrugged. "Okay, so if not in a UFO, where did he go?"

"I don't know," Jonah said. "But I'm going to find out."

Jonah didn't know how he would find out; he only knew that he would. It would be easier, he thought, if his mother helped. But so far, the only person besides Jonah who seemed to believe that Mr. Rosetti was even missing was Granville.

On the way home, Jonah stopped at Mr. Rosetti's house and rang the bell. He rang it even though he already knew that nobody would answer. Today's *Chronicle* was on the front porch, along with the rest of the newspapers.

As the door chime echoed inside the house, Jonah began to gather the rolled papers. He stacked them, like logs, in a corner of the porch. Then he went around the side of the house and let himself into the backyard.

Jonah picked up the garbage can lids and replaced them on the cans. Then he picked up Mr. Rosetti's rake and shovel. He took them to the garage and opened the door.

Jonah was startled. Right in front of him was Mr. Rosetti's car. Jonah had forgotten about Mr. Rosetti's car. It was very shiny. It was always very shiny. Jonah thought Mr. Rosetti spent more time keeping his car shiny than he did driving it.

In his mind Jonah got a picture of Mr. Rosetti polishing his car. He could even hear Mr. Rosetti's voice. "This car has to last me," Mr. Rosetti would say.

Jonah set the tools against a wall and walked around the car. It made him slightly nervous to be walking around alone in Mr. Rosetti's garage.

He almost expected Mr. Rosetti to pop up from somewhere and say, "Why, hello there, Jonah." But he didn't.

Before going home, Jonah stopped again on Mr. Rosetti's front porch. This time he didn't ring the bell. He opened Mr. Rosetti's mailbox and pulled out the mail. It was a big stack. He took it with him when he went home.

four

"Woz is dead, and it's Jonah's fault!" Todd said. He said this as he and Jonah stood in their father's kitchen on Friday night making Swedish meatballs.

Cooking dinner together was Jonah's favorite part about these alternate weekend visits with their father. Why did Todd have to mention Woz right now? He hadn't spoken of Woz during the long drive through heavy traffic to their father's condominium. Nor had Todd mentioned Woz during their trip to the grocery store. Jonah suspected that Todd had chosen this exact moment to tell about Woz on purpose. Just to spoil things for Jonah.

"Woz isn't dead," Jonah said. "He's only missing."

"He's dead," Todd said confidently. "Otherwise, he would have shown up."

"Wait a minute," Mr. Twist said. "Somebody had better begin at the beginning and tell me what happened."

Todd began. He told about how he had come home from school the day before and found the door to his room ajar. He told how the door to Woz's cage was popped open and Woz was gone. And he told about finding Mrs. Einstein asleep on the top of Woz's cage.

"And Mrs. Einstein looks very fat," Todd said. "Suspiciously fat."

"Uh-oh," Mr. Twist said. "Could Mrs. Einstein have eaten Woz?"

"No!" Jonah said. "Mrs. Einstein is too little. She's hardly any bigger than Woz is. Besides, there weren't any bones. I don't think Mrs. Einstein would want the bones." Then he added, "Or the fur."

He didn't know whether these facts would mean the same thing to his father as they did to him. But for Jonah, the lack of bones and fur were telling.

"Hmmm . . ." Mr. Twist said. He picked up an egg from the counter and broke it into the bowl of bread crumbs.

"I think she did eat Woz, bones and all," Todd said. "Or at least she killed Woz and left the body somewhere. Cats have killed hamsters before, you know." He sounded upset, and looked as though he might be crying. But he was also cutting an onion, which Jonah knew could lead to the same thing.

Mr. Twist said, "There's something I don't understand. Who left the door to your room open, and who opened Woz's cage?"

"The cat, of course," Todd answered. "That's obvious."

"She didn't," Jonah protested. "At least she didn't open the door to your room. You left it open yourself. Every day this week. I know, because after school I kept finding Mrs. Einstein asleep on Woz's cage!"

"See!" Todd crowed. "She's been stalking Woz. I told you!"

Jonah moaned. He hadn't meant to tell about finding Mrs. Einstein asleep on Woz's cage. Why couldn't he keep his mouth shut?

"And how did the cage door get open?" Mr. Twist asked.

"Woz opened it?" Jonah said hopefully. The truth was that when Jonah tried to imagine Woz working the cage door open with his little paws, he couldn't. But he *could* imagine Mrs. Einstein doing it. He had seen her shove her paws between the couch cushions in order to reach the felt mouse she'd lost. She could have opened the door to Woz's cage.

Todd snorted. "I had Woz for three years and he never even tried to get his door open. Mrs. Einstein has been in the house a week and now Woz is gone. Anybody could figure out Mrs. Einstein opened the cage, not Woz."

Mr. Twist dumped a package of ground beef into the bowl with the bread crumbs and egg. "Have you looked around the house for Woz?" he asked.

"Sure," Todd said. "But it was no use. I told you, he's dead." He scooped up the onions he had chopped and dumped them into the bowl with the meat.

"I think he's hiding," Jonah said. "And Mom says I might be right." Jonah washed his hands at the sink. His part in making the meatballs was about to begin. "Anyway, Mom says we have to keep Mrs. Einstein locked up until we find Woz, just in case."

Jonah didn't like to think about Mrs. Einstein being locked up. Mrs. Twist had put the kitten and her food dishes in the bathroom with the litter box. Now the only time Jonah saw Mrs. Einstein was when he had to use the bathroom, which wasn't as often as he wished. But frequently, as he passed by the bathroom door, he heard Mrs. Einstein mewing. It gave him a lump in his throat every time he thought about it.

"Well, I'm very sorry that Woz is missing," Mr. Twist said. "But I suggest that you keep looking. There are a great many places a hamster could hide in a house."

"That's what I think," Jonah said.

"Well, I don't," Todd said. "Woz is dead, and looking for him is a waste of time."

Mr. Twist shoved the mixing bowl over in front of Jonah.

"Okay," he said, "do your thing."

Jonah plunged his hands into the bowl and began squishing. As he squished, the meat began to blend with the rest of the mix.

Jonah watched his work carefully. He knew that he would be done mixing when everything was the same color. When it was, he started on the meatballs. He rolled globs of meat around in his palms until they were as round and regular as ping-pong balls. Then he stacked them neatly.

Stacking the meatballs was Jonah's favorite part. He liked to make the stacks look like the piles of cannonballs at Fort Point. It took a long time, but Jonah was proud of his work when he was done.

"What would you two like to do after dinner?" Mr. Twist asked as he dropped the first of the meatballs into sizzling butter.

"Go bowling!" Jonah said. The stacks of meatballs had reminded him of bowling, though he wasn't sure how.

"Well," Todd said, "I *should* do some homework for my Spanish class, but I feel too upset about Woz to work tonight. So I'd like to do something fun—like rent a movie." He looked meaningfully at Jonah.

Jonah sighed. Woz's disappearance was really making things tough. He hoped they could find Woz soon. "I guess a movie is okay," he said. Even as he said it, he was pretty sure Todd would be the person who chose the movie.

The smell of the frying meatballs made Jonah's mouth water. He was getting very hungry. He wondered whether Woz was hungry, wherever he was. Or had he stuffed his cheeks with sunflower seeds before he left the cage?

Sunflower seeds. In his mind, Jonah got a picture of Woz holding a sunflower seed in his paws. He would turn it over and over and then crack the shell with his teeth. Then he'd drop the husk as he popped the nutmeat into his mouth. If Woz were hiding somewhere, he would really want to have sunflower seeds to eat.

That was it! Jonah could scatter sunflower seeds around the house. Then, if Woz was hungry, he could have something to eat while he was waiting to be found.

Even better, if the sunflower seeds disappeared, Jonah would know for certain that Woz was still alive.

Jonah looked at his father standing over the pan of frying meatballs. He was eager to tell him about the plan. But Todd was standing nearby. Knowing Todd, he'd say that Jonah's plan was dumb. Jonah pinched his lips together.

For a change you kept your mouth shut, he said to himself.

The movie Todd chose had a lot of jet fighters in it. But it also had a lot of kissing. Jonah would have preferred a cartoon, or a movie about animals. He wasn't sorry when his bedtime came.

This week it was Jonah's turn to sleep in the bottom bunk. Usually, he liked the top bunk best, but the bottom had one advantage: He could open his drawer of toys under the bunk without getting out of bed.

Jonah reached down and rolled the drawer open. He felt around until his fingers fastened on a familiar object. A Transformer. In the dim glow of street lights through the blinds, he changed the toy from a jet to a robot and back again as he drifted off to sleep.

Sometime later Jonah awoke with a start. His

chest was pounding and he felt sweaty all over. He'd had a dream. In it, a robot had transformed itself into Mr. Rosetti. This Mr. Rosetti was no bigger than Mrs. Einstein, and the two of them were talking together about the disappearance of Woz. Next, they were joined by an army camouflage jet fighter that promptly transformed itself into Granville. Granville was wearing camouflage fatigues, full dress. Together, Granville, Mr. Rosetti, and Mrs. Einstein marched off in search of Woz.

Jonah needed a drink of water. In the bathroom he ran the water until it was very cold, then he took great gulps. As he padded back up the hall, he saw that a light was still on in the living room.

Mr. Twist was sitting in the large, nubbly tweed armchair with his feet on the ottoman. A book was open in his lap. His mouth was also open, and out of it came gentle rumbling noises. Mr. Twist was asleep.

"Dad?" Jonah said. He shook his father's shoulder. "Dad, wake up."

"Huh?" Mr. Twist blinked his eyes open. "What's wrong?"

"You were asleep."

"Ah, you noticed," his father said. "Happens every time. I just want to read a chapter or so of my book before bed, and I fall asleep. Then I wake up with a crick in my neck."

"You should try reading in bed," Jonah suggested.

Mr. Twist chuckled and rubbed his neck. "Too easy," he said. "But why are you up, Jonah?"

"I had a dream," Jonah said.

"A bad dream?" his father asked.

Jonah considered. "Not really," he answered. "But not a good dream either. Just weird."

"Do you want to tell me about it?"

"Naw." Jonah squeezed into the armchair next to his father. "But I do want to tell you about something else. A plan. It's about Woz."

Jonah told his father about the sunflower seeds and how he would be able to tell if Woz was still alive if the seeds were eaten.

"Good idea," Mr. Twist said.

"Yeah," Jonah said. "I've been getting a lot of them lately. Ideas, that is. I think it's because of Mrs. Einstein."

"And how would that work?" his father asked.

"Well, it's because Mrs. Einstein might be smart," Jonah said. "I think it's rubbing off on me."

"Could be," Mr. Twist said. "Or it could be something else."

"Like what?" Jonah asked.

"Like it could be that you've always had good ideas, but just never noticed it until now. Maybe it's your good report card that rubbed off on you."

Jonah gave his father a puzzled look. "Is this something about public relations?" he asked. Mr. Twist's job was in public relations.

Mr. Twist laughed. "In a way," he said. "Your own personal public relations. A good report card can give you confidence, and a little confidence goes a long way toward helping a person notice he has good ideas."

"Huh," Jonah said. He wasn't sure he understood what his father meant, but he liked the way it sounded.

"I just wish I could get a good idea about Mr. Rosetti," Jonah said. "He's missing, and I can't figure out where he could be. Granville thinks maybe he went in a UFO, but I don't."

"It's doubtful," Mr. Twist said. He asked Jonah to tell him about Mr. Rosetti's disappearance.

Then Mr. Twist said, "I'm sure there's a reasonable explanation, Jonah. People don't just vanish."

"That's the trouble," Jonah said. "Everyone says the same thing, but Mr. Rosetti is still gone.

"Mom said she'd help, but all she did so far was call Granville's mother. Then Mrs. Jones used Mr. Rosetti's spare key and went into his house. She said everything looked 'perfectly normal.' So now Mom is more sure than ever that Mr. Rosetti went on vacation. But I still think he's missing." Jonah sighed. "I collect his mail every day."

"Well, be patient," his father said. "He's bound to turn up. Doesn't he have a sister in Portland? Maybe he went to visit her."

"I don't think so," Jonah said. "Mr. Rosetti can't stand his sister in Portland. She's worse than Todd."

Mr. Twist laughed. "That bad, huh?" he asked.

"Worse," Jonah said.

"Well, wherever Mr. Rosetti is, I don't think he's gone for good. So remember that, okay, Jonah?"

"I'll try," Jonah said.

Mr. Twist closed his book and set it on the table beside his chair. He squeezed Jonah around the shoulder. "I think it's time both of us got some sleep, don't you?"

"I suppose," Jonah said.

He waited while his father turned out the light, then they walked down the dark hall together.

At the door to his room Jonah stopped. "I just

remembered something," he whispered.

"What's that, Jonah?"

"I'm supposed to ask if you can take me and Granville and Juliet Fisher to see some elephant seals next Saturday. It's for social studies."

"Well," his father said. "I'll have to give it some thought, but I can probably manage it. Who is this Juliet Fisher?"

"She's a real pain," Jonah said. Thinking about people who had disappeared reminded him of Juliet. It seemed to him that the wrong people were turning up missing.

"Is she a backseat driver?" his father asked.

"I don't know," Jonah said, "but probably. She's very bossy."

"The only elephant seals are at Point Año Nuevo, and it's a long drive. I may have to ask Miss Fisher to sit in front to prevent her from being a backseat driver. But I think I can handle her."

"I hope so," Jonah said. He thought it would take a grown-up like his father or Mrs. Lacey to handle Juliet. So far, he and Granville had failed.

"Elephant seals are huge, you know," Mr. Twist said.

"I know," Jonah said.

"You should have held out for an elephant seal for a pet," his father said.

Jonah laughed. "I don't think it's allowed," he said.

"I'm sure it's not," said Mr. Twist. "But wouldn't your mother have been surprised."

five

GRANVILLE, his binder tucked under his arm, was standing in line in front of Jonah at the door to Room 4B. Jonah leaned over and said, "When we get to the library, just follow Juliet. She'll lead us to the right books."

"Got it," Granville said.

Jonah had learned about Juliet and libraries way back in kindergarten. Then, he followed her to the picture book section. Without someone to follow, Jonah often got distracted by all the books and never got where he was going at all. But Juliet Fisher must have been born in a library. She never got lost.

"The first five groups will walk themselves to the library," Mrs. Lacey said. "I want you to use your best library behavior. And if you need help, speak to Ms. Garrett." She put her hand on the doorknob. "And one more thing—no talking in the halls. Not a sound. Understand?"

"Yes, Mrs. Lacey," fifteen third graders chorused.

As soon as the door had closed behind them, Granville turned around. He walked backward down the hall. He crossed his eyes and flared his nostrils at Jonah. He leaned sideways and wiggled his fingers at the kids in back of Jonah. He walked with wobbly knees. He hopped like a backward rabbit.

Jonah covered his mouth to keep from laughing. Down the line there were a few muffled giggles. Nobody else made a sound. But as soon as the group got inside the library, everyone behind Granville burst out laughing. Everyone, that is, except Juliet.

"You're going to be in trouble," she said to Granville.

"Me?" Granville asked with an innocent grin. "Why?"

"You made everyone laugh," Juliet said.

"Nobody makes anyone laugh," Granville said. "People laugh if they feel like it. It's like sneezing."

"Mrs. Lacey wouldn't say that," Juliet said.

Granville shrugged. "Mrs. Lacey isn't here," he said.

"But someone might tell her," Juliet said. She looked hard at Granville and added, "Someone should."

"Like you, I suppose," Granville said. "Juliet

Busybody Fisher, minding everyone else's business."

Some girls who were standing nearby snickered. But Jonah wasn't laughing anymore. He was worrying. "I think we should get some books," he said. He put his binder on a table by an empty seat.

"Right," Granville said. He set his binder at the seat next to Jonah's. "Lead the way, Juliet," he said. "We need some books on elephant seals."

"Find them yourself," Juliet said. She slapped her binder onto the table and sat down. She folded her arms across her chest. Juliet didn't look like she was going anywhere.

"That's fine with us," Granville said. "In fact, if you want to quit our group, that's fine, too. It wasn't our idea to work with you, you know."

"Well, it wasn't mine, either, you know!" Juliet said hotly. She turned away and stared at the wall.

Jonah felt a rising sense of panic. He didn't want to work with Juliet, but she would have been a help in finding the books. "Now what?" he asked Granville.

"No sweat," Granville said. "Follow me."

Granville walked up to Ms. Garrett's desk. Jonah was right behind him.

"We need some books on elephant seals," Granville said. "Can you show us where they are?"

"I can do better than that," Ms. Garrett said. "I can show you how to find them yourself." She pushed back her chair and walked over to the card catalog.

Jonah's heart sank. The card catalog was one of the most mysterious places in the whole library. Mysterious and scary. He knew it was one of the things he would never figure out.

"Do you know how to use a card catalog?" Ms. Garret asked.

"No," Jonah said gloomily.

"Nope!" Granville said brightly.

"First, you need to know how to spell what you're looking for," Ms. Garrett said.

That lets me out, Jonah thought. Spelling was not one of the things he was good at.

"We're looking for seals," Granville said. "Elephant seals. S-E-A-L-S."

"Good!" Ms. Garrett said. "Now watch carefully." She showed them how to find the card about seals. Then she showed them the number on the card. Then she wrote the number on a scrap of paper and led Granville and Jonah to the place on the shelf that had the same number.

"See?" she said. "It's easy."

"A snap!" Granville said.

Impossible, Jonah thought. Jonah was sure he could never do it on his own. Following Juliet was much easier.

Just as though she had read his mind, Ms. Garrett said to Jonah, "Don't worry if you didn't get it on the first try. By the end of sixth grade you'll be an expert."

Jonah doubted it. He followed Granville back to their seats in a kind of fog.

"Hey!" Granville said. "Juliet's gone. She quit!"

Jonah looked around. "I don't think so," he said. Juliet's binder was still on the table.

Jonah and Granville sat down. They looked around uneasily.

"Where do you think she went?" Granville asked.

"I don't know," Jonah said.

"Maybe to Mrs. Lacey," Granville said, "to tell about the laughing."

"Maybe," Jonah said. He opened one of the books and began looking for elephant seals. But he also watched for Juliet. He didn't want to be in trouble with Mrs. Lacey for bad library behavior. Jonah grew more anxious by the minute.

Finally, Juliet returned. She sat down without

speaking. She looked bright in the eyes, like someone who might be mad.

"Where were you?" Granville asked.

"None of your business," Juliet said.

Granville shrugged. "Okay," he said. "You don't have to tell me. You don't have to help us read about elephant seals either if you don't want to. In fact, it's all right if you leave again."

Juliet scowled steadily at Granville for several seconds without saying anything. Then she said, "You want me to quit. I already figured that out. But if I quit, I'll get an F on this report. And I'm not going to get any F's just because of you two!"

Juliet opened her binder and turned to a place in the middle. She snapped the rings open and pulled out a piece of paper.

"Here's the list of things we're supposed to find out before we do our observations. 'Natural history,' " she read. "You look that up," she ordered Granville.

She took another book and shoved it toward Jonah. "You look up 'range,' " she said. "That's wherever the animal lives in the world.

"And I'm going to do 'diet,' " she said finally. "My mother's the dietitian at Community Hospital, so I know a lot about food."

Juliet opened a book and began reading.

Jonah slumped down in his seat. Now what? he wondered. He turned to look at Granville. Granville was also slumped in his seat.

"Guess we might as well read," Granville muttered.

Jonah found the page about elephant seals. He studied the pictures for a long time. Finally, he leaned over to Granville and said, "Guess what? Elephant seals are really ugly."

Granville shook his head. "You're telling me!" he said.

When the three o'clock bell rang, Granville stayed after school. So did Jonah. Mrs. Lacey had invited them to.

As the other kids filed out of the room, Jonah sat at his desk thinking. What if Mrs. Lacey sent home a note? What if Jonah's mother got mad about the note and said he couldn't keep Mrs. Einstein?

"Juliet must have told about how I acted in the hall," Granville said.

"Yeah," Jonah agreed, "and how I laughed in the library."

"I think we're in trouble," Granville said.

"I think you're right," Jonah said.

Jonah could already see his mother reading the note. He could hear her voice. "Responsible people don't act up in the library," she would say. "I don't think you're responsible enough to have a pet, Jonah."

"Boys," Mrs. Lacey said, "I'm ready to talk to you now."

Jonah and Granville marched up to Mrs. Lacey's desk. As soon as they got there, Granville began talking.

"You said not to make any noise in the hall," he said. "And I didn't. But I never heard any rules about walking backward or making faces. Or hopping, either. And I didn't make people laugh. They laughed because they felt like it. They thought it was funny. And anyhow, Jonah wasn't the only one who laughed when we got to the library. Everyone else did, too. Everyone except Juliet, that is."

Boy, Jonah thought. That Granville Jones really had guts! And he had even stuck up for Jonah. What a great friend! He grinned at Mrs. Lacey.

Mrs. Lacey looked at Jonah. Then she looked back at Granville. Then a bemused smile edged itself across her face.

"That's very interesting," she said. "I'm surprised that nobody told me you had misbehaved in the hall, Granville. You must have a lot of friends in this class."

Granville gulped. The gulp was so loud Jonah could hear it. "Nobody told?" Granville asked.

"No."

"Then why. . ."

"Not everyone has as many friends in this class as you do, Granville," Mrs. Lacey said. "Juliet Fisher, for instance, doesn't have many friends."

"She has zero friends," Jonah said. He wanted to add that it was Juliet's fault that she had no friends, but something warned him against it.

"Exactly," Mrs. Lacey said. "So you can imagine how sorry I was to hear she was crying in the girls' room when she was supposed to be working in the library."

"She was crying?" Granville asked.

"So I'm told," Mrs. Lacey said.

"Oh," Jonah said. Thinking of Juliet crying gave Jonah a strange feeling. He couldn't identify the feeling, but it wasn't good.

Mrs. Lacey picked up a stack of spelling papers on her desk. She neatened the edges and stuck them into her grade book. Then she reached under the desk for her briefcase.

"Now, I know Juliet isn't always the easiest person in the world to get along with . . ." she said.

"That's the truth!" Granville said.

". . . but she does want to have friends," Mrs. Lacey continued. "And I think that if you two would give her a chance, you would find that she's a good partner. She might even turn out to be a friend."

"Hmmm . . ." Granville said. He looked doubtful.

Jonah tried to get a picture in his head of Juliet doing something that a friend might do. He couldn't.

"So I'd like to count on you two to make Juliet feel welcome in your group. Can I do that?" Mrs. Lacey asked.

Jonah and Granville exchanged a bleak look. Then they looked back at Mrs. Lacey. She brushed a clump of gray hair back from her forehead and smiled at them. She didn't seem to be in any hurry for an answer. In fact, Jonah had the impression she would wait there all afternoon until she got the answer she wanted.

Jonah sighed. "I guess so," he said at last.

"Okay," Granville grumbled.

"Wonderful," Mrs. Lacey beamed. "You're both such nice boys, I knew you'd understand."

Just as they were leaving the room, Mrs. Lacey called after them. "Oh, and Granville," she said. "Just one more thing. I want to thank you for owning up to your bad behavior in the hall. I'm sure you won't repeat it."

Granville burst out the front door of Mills Elementary School. Then he leapt the five steps to the ground. He smacked his head with the palm of his hand.

"Dumb!" he said. "I'm so dumb. I thought she had the goods on me so I confessed. But I didn't have to! How could I be so dumb?"

Jonah thought. "I've been trying to learn to keep my mouth shut," he said. "Maybe you should, too."

Granville laughed. "Yeah," he said. "Maybe so. All I know is we're stuck with Juliet for good now."

"True," Jonah said. "And now Juliet is the boss."

"Aaaghhh," Granville said. "Don't remind me!" He sprinted away in the direction of home.

Jonah tagged behind with his lunch box in hand. He lost sight of Granville for a while, but as he turned onto Manzanita Avenue he heard Granville's voice.

"Hey, Jonah. Up here."

Jonah looked up. There was Granville stretched out along the branch of a liquidambar tree.

"You might say Juliet Fisher drives me up a tree," Granville said.

Jonah laughed. Then he had another thought. "You're not going to jump on her, are you?" he asked. He could remember when Granville had jumped out of trees at him.

"Naw," Granville said. "Especially not if she's going to cry."

Thinking of Juliet crying gave Jonah a bad feeling again. "I didn't think she'd cry," Jonah said.

Granville was quiet for a moment. Then he did a hanging somersault from the tree and landed softly on the ground. "Me, neither," he said. "I didn't think she'd cry."

Granville hitched up his camouflage pants. He tucked in a corner of his T-shirt. Then he ducked behind a bush and came back with his backpack.

"There's something else," he said.

"What's that?" Jonah asked.

"Mrs. Lacey. She's spooky."

"She is," Jonah agreed. "Very."

six

THE DOOR to the bathroom was closed, so Jonah knocked. Nobody answered. Jonah listened carefully. He heard a mewing. Then a spotted paw stuck out from under the bathroom door.

Cautiously, Jonah opened the door. "Hello, Mrs. Einstein," he said. He closed the door behind him as he went in.

Mrs. Einstein purred when Jonah picked her up. She climbed up Jonah's shirt and snuffled around his ear. Then she took a clump of Jonah's hair in her mouth and pulled hard.

"Ouch!" Jonah said. He lifted the purring kitten off his shoulder and sat her on the floor. "You must be mad at me," he said. "Or maybe you just want to be let out." He stroked her back.

"I only wish Woz wasn't lost. Then you *could* be out."

Jonah liked to visit with Mrs. Einstein after school. But Todd had begun to complain. He said that Jonah was always in the bathroom. He said there was no reason for Jonah to always be in the bathroom. To Todd, always was two days.

Jonah's reason was Mrs. Einstein. But he needed a better reason for Todd and his mother. Today, he thought he had one.

Jonah put the stopper in the tub and ran the water. When the tub was full, Jonah put in his wind-up frog and his speedboat. He also put in a long, flexible plastic tube and some water balloons. Then he stripped off his clothes and climbed in.

"I've had a hard day," he said to Mrs. Einstein. "All I want is a nice, long, relaxing bath." This was something Jonah's mother often said.

The truth was that Jonah didn't think baths were nice at all. Especially not long ones. He thought they were a nuisance. Still, if he was going to spend the rest of the afternoon in the bathtub, he needed a reason his mother would understand. He wound up the frog and watched as it kicked through the water.

Mrs. Einstein sat on the toilet seat while Jonah was in the tub. Jonah talked to her. "Our plan for getting rid of Juliet Fisher was a major flop," he said. "Now Juliet bosses us all the time. She made Granville take notes. And she made me draw a map."

Actually, Jonah had rather enjoyed drawing

the map. But it bothered him that Juliet had ordered him to.

Jonah took the plastic tube and blew bubbles behind the speedboat. The bubbles pushed the speedboat through the water. It wasn't speedy, but it did move. Mrs. Einstein cocked her head to one side and then the other as she watched.

"And Dad is going to take me and Granville and Juliet to see the elephant seals next Saturday," Jonah went on. "It's a long ride in the car, and I don't even want to see elephant seals. They're so ugly. If you saw their pictures, you'd know. I'd rather see a rattlesnake."

He blew hard on the tube and the speedboat bounced a little as it moved.

Todd knocked on the bathroom door. "Is someone in there?" he called.

"Me!" Jonah answered.

"I should have known," Todd said. "Well, you'll have to come out. I need the bathroom."

"Can't," Jonah called.

"Why not?" Todd asked. "As if I didn't know . . ."

"I'm in the tub," Jonah called.

"You're *what*?" Todd opened the bathroom door and stuck his head in. "You *are* in the tub. I don't believe it. Now what am I supposed to do?"

"You only have to move Mrs. Einstein from the toilet seat," Jonah said.

"No thanks," Todd said. "I'll hold it."

"Well, I might be here a long time," Jonah said. "Maybe you should use a bush."

"Great," Todd said. "That's just great." He slammed the door as he left.

Jonah took a green water balloon and filled it half full with water. Then he filled it the rest of the way with air. It floated, half submerged, in the tub.

Mrs. Einstein hopped to the rim of the tub. She looked curiously at the balloon.

"Watch this," Jonah said. "That's the Loch Ness Monster, and the guys in the boat have to capture it." Jonah blew through the tube again, edging the speedboat around the floating monster.

Mrs. Einstein stretched a paw toward the bubbles. She tried to bat them as they popped. Jonah blew bubbles under the monster. It bobbed up and down in the water.

The kitten reached for the balloon. As her claw touched it, the balloon burst with a bang. Mrs. Einstein leapt into the air and, spinning, landed with a splash in the tub.

"Oh, no!" Jonah grabbed the wildly struggling

kitten and pulled her to safety. Then he climbed from the tub and wrapped the kitten in a towel. It was a very big towel and she was a very little kitten. When he was done, Jonah had a bundle bigger than a basketball. Only the tip of Mrs. Einstein's nose peeked out.

"Jonah!" Mrs. Twist's voice clattered up the stairs. "Jonah Twist, come down here!"

"I can't," Jonah hollered.

"Now!" his mother boomed. She sounded very angry.

Jonah took another towel and wrapped it around his waist. Clutching it with one hand, and the bundled kitten with the other, he dripped his way downstairs.

"Jonah, what is the meaning of this?" Mrs. Twist stood in the living room. She held a broom in one hand. In the other hand she held a dustpan. In the dustpan were sunflower seeds.

"I've been finding sunflower seeds all over the house for two days," she said. "I sweep them up, but every time I turn around there are more. Todd says he's not responsible, so I figure that leaves you."

"Oh," Jonah said.

" 'Oh,' what?" Mrs. Twist said. "Jonah, I want an explanation."

Jonah clutched his towel more tightly around his waist. "I thought Woz was eating them," he said.

"Woz is gone. You can't tell me that a hamster who isn't even here has been spreading sunflower seeds all over the house!" Mrs. Twist's voice was getting higher.

"No. I did that," Jonah admitted.

"That's what I thought," his mother said.

"But I thought Woz was eating them. I didn't know you were sweeping them up." Jonah sighed. Just yesterday he had noticed that the seeds in his mother's bedroom were gone. It had made him happy to think that Woz might have found the seeds.

"So you've been scattering seeds around for Woz?" his mother said.

"I guess so," Jonah said.

"Well, I want you to stop."

"But Woz might be hungry!" Jonah protested.

"Jonah," his mother said, "Woz has been gone for several days now. I think it's very unlikely we're going to see him again. And we can't leave seeds all over the house. They might attract rodents."

"Woz *is* a rodent," Jonah said. That was the point.

"So are rats," his mother said. "And Jonah"—
she measured each word out carefully—"I abso-
lutely cannot stand rats. Got it?"

"Got it," Jonah said.

"That's good." His mother sighed. "And now,
Jonah, perhaps you'd like to tell me why you're
dripping on my rug."

Jonah looked at his feet. There were little dark
water stains on the surrounding carpet.

"Because you called me?" Jonah ventured. He
wasn't sure he was up to another round of
questioning.

"Jonah . . ."

"Okay, okay. It's because I was taking a bath. I
was putting Mrs. Einstein in a towel when you
called."

As if in response to her name, Mrs. Einstein
mewed.

Jonah's mother stared at the bundled towel
under Jonah's arm. She bent over and peered in
the hole where Mrs. Einstein's nose was showing. Then she fixed Jonah with a puzzled look.

"Why were you . . .?" She stopped. "Never
mind. I'm not sure I want to know why you were
taking a bath in the middle of the afternoon."

"That's good," Jonah muttered.

"But it's not a good idea to bathe a kitten," his

mother continued. "She could get chilled, and then she might catch cold."

"Oh," Jonah said. He started to say that getting Mrs. Einstein wet was a mistake, but stopped himself. He didn't think this was the right time for his mother to hear about more of his mistakes.

"I'll go dry her off," he said.

"A good idea," Mrs. Twist said.

Jonah put the bundled Mrs. Einstein on his bed while he toweled off and quickly dressed. Then he went to his mother's room for the hair dryer.

Mrs. Einstein had wormed her way out of the towel when Jonah returned. Her fur stood out in damp spikes all over her body. And she looked even smaller. Far too small, Jonah noted, to have eaten as much as half a hamster.

Mrs. Einstein trembled at first as Jonah brushed and blow-dried her fur. But after a bit she stopped trembling and started purring. She even took a few licks at her paws and chest.

"I've been making a lot of plans lately," Jonah said. "But even when I remember them, they turn out crummy."

Jonah felt especially unlucky about the sun-flower seed plan; it had ended in his being grilled by his mother. He hated it when she asked a lot of questions. What he hated most were the answers he had to give.

As he thought about it, Jonah realized he had a few questions of his own. Why, for instance, did Mrs. Einstein have to stay locked up if his mother was so certain that Woz was gone for good? Why was it that nobody believed Woz was coming back? And why wouldn't anyone believe that Mr. Rosetti was missing?

Jonah was unusually quiet during dinnertime that night. It was often hard to get a word in edgewise during dinner; Todd liked to do all the talking. And mainly he talked about how great he was doing in school. This time Jonah didn't care. He had things on his mind.

Like the sunflower seed plan. It still seemed to him that it was a pretty good plan. The unlucky part was that his mother had swept up the seeds. But suppose he put the seeds in places where his mother wouldn't see them?

Mrs. Twist often said that she didn't have time to clean the house "like it should be cleaned." Jonah knew what that meant. It meant that most times she didn't clean under the furniture. Suppose Jonah hid the seeds under the furniture where his mother wouldn't find them?

Suppose, moreover, that he put only a certain number of seeds in each place. Say, five. Then he could check and tell for sure if Woz was eating them.

Jonah began to like the shape of this plan. It was much better than the old one. There was, as far as he could tell, only one other problem. Rats. Even Jonah would be upset if rats moved in.

Jonah thought about his house. He knew it was built on a concrete slab. He also knew that the sides were stucco. "Any rat that wanted to get in here would break its teeth," Jonah said.

"What?" his mother asked.

"Nothing," Jonah said. He hadn't meant to speak out loud.

"He's talking to himself," Todd said. "He does that a lot lately. I hear him in the bathroom."

After dinner, Jonah cleared his plate. While his mother put away the leftovers, Jonah scraped the plates. Then, while his mother filled the sink with sudsy water, Jonah watched by her side.

"Jonah," Mrs. Twist said at last, "I appreciate the help, but shouldn't you be doing homework?"

"I will soon," Jonah said. He watched as his mother washed and rinsed a plate.

"Mom," he said, "did you find out about Mr. Rosetti?"

"Oh, Jonah," his mother said, "you're not going to start on Mr. Rosetti again, are you?"

Jonah took a deep breath. "But you promised," he said. "You didn't keep your promise."

Mrs. Twist looked startled. She reached out and turned off the spigot. Then she wiped her hands on a towel. "You're right," she said. "I did promise. And I didn't do a good enough job of keeping that promise."

Jonah's mother sat back down at the dining table. Jonah took the seat across from her. His mother folded her hands and looked solemn. Jonah folded his hands, too.

"I did ask around," his mother said. "None of the neighbors has seen Mr. Rosetti."

"Of course not!" Jonah said. "He's missing!"

"Most people seem to think he went on a trip," Mrs. Twist continued. "Twice someone mentioned a sister in Portland."

"I know about her," Jonah said. "Mr. Rosetti isn't there."

"Now, Jonah," his mother said, "you can't be sure of that."

"I'm sure," Jonah said firmly. "Mr. Rosetti doesn't like his sister."

"Well, that's no reason," Mrs. Twist said. "Sometimes you don't like Todd very much, but you'll go visit him when you're grown up, won't you?"

Jonah thought about this. He decided not to answer the question.

"There's another reason," he said. "Every day I collect Mr. Rosetti's mail, and there are two letters from some lady in Portland."

"Good heavens. I never thought of the mail!" his mother said. "Jonah, I think I'd better have a look at that stack of mail."

Jonah ran to the hall table and returned with Mr. Rosetti's mail. It was a whole armload now.

Mrs. Twist sorted through it. She put the advertisements in one pile, the bills in another, and the personal letters in a third. The third pile contained only two letters. They were both from Portland.

"This is very odd," she said.

"That's what I think," Jonah said. "I don't think his sister would write to Mr. Rosetti if he was at her house, do you?"

"No, I don't," his mother said. Then she looked hard at Jonah. "What I do think, though, is that you are very smart. And I also think I had better telephone this woman in Portland."

Jonah watched as his mother went to the phone and dialed long-distance information. He listened as she asked for a number of a Mrs. Violet Martinez. And he listened some more while she talked to Mrs. Martinez.

First Jonah's mother did most of the talking. She explained that Jonah and Mr. Rosetti were friends, and that Jonah was worried. She told everything, even about the spade.

Then Mrs. Martinez must have begun talking because his mother said, "Uh-huh," several times.

Then she said, "I see."

Then she said, "Oh, dear."

When she hung up the phone, Jonah's mother wore her most worried expression. "That was Mr. Rosetti's sister, all right," Mrs. Twist said. "She says she has been writing to tell her brother she will be coming for a visit next week. She says she thought the reason he hadn't answered might be that he didn't want her to come."

"That would be true if he had gotten his mail," Jonah said. He was pretty sure Mr. Rosetti wouldn't enjoy a visit from his sister. But then, where . . .? Jonah got a picture in his mind of a UFO.

"Well," his mother said, "I have promised Mrs. Violet Martinez that I will call her back." She put her hands on Jonah's shoulders. "But first," she said, "I have to telephone the police."

seven

ON SATURDAY Juliet rode beside Mr. Twist in the front seat. Jonah and Granville rode in back. It was a warm day for November, sparkling and still.

Jonah could just see Juliet's yellow rain hat above the front seat. He couldn't see her slicker, or her boots, or her umbrella, or her checked woolen scarf. But he knew they were there. He'd seen them when she got in the car.

"You're welcome to take off your raincoat and hat," Mr. Twist said to Juliet.

"That's all right," Juliet said.

"I think you might be more comfortable if you took them off," he persisted. "It's a long ride."

"I am comfortable, thank you," Juliet said. "Besides, I'd just have to put them back on when we get there."

Mr. Twist leaned forward over the steering wheel and scanned the sky. "Hmmm," he said. "It looks clear to me. And the forecast calls for sun for the next three days. I don't think you'll be needing rain gear today, Juliet."

"But you can never be sure," Juliet said. "The tickets say the tour takes place even if it's rainy. And that you should come prepared. So I did. Anyway, Mr. Twist, I hate to get rained on. I really, really hate it. And I refuse to get wet just because *some* people wanted to study yucky elephant seals."

"I see," Jonah's father said. Jonah recognized his father's tone of voice. It was the one he used when he really didn't see at all.

"I'm prepared, too," Granville said. "Just not for rain." He was wearing his camouflage fatigues, his helmet, a canteen on a belt, a walkie-talkie on another belt, and combat boots. His face was smudged with black charcoal.

"Yes, I noticed you're prepared." Mr. Twist laughed. "But for what, Granville? This is billed as a nature tour, not a war."

"Prepared to blend in," Granville said. "See, I figure I can get closer to the elephant seals if I blend in with the background. Then I can study them better. Makes sense, huh?"

"Well, up to a point, Granville. I went on this tour once myself, and—ahem—you may find it harder to blend in than you imagine."

"That's okay," Granville said confidently. "I'm an expert."

Jonah surveyed his own clothes. He was wearing blue jeans and a faded red sweatshirt that said "Stanford University" on it. Todd had given Jonah the sweatshirt. Todd said it was worn-out and he didn't want it anymore.

Jonah thought that in a red sweatshirt he was unlikely to blend in with anything. And also unlikely to stay dry if it rained. Not that Jonah minded getting wet. He didn't. He just wished he'd thought to get prepared in some special way. A baseball cap would have been good.

"I *would* have been prepared," Jonah said, "but I forgot."

"That's okay," his father said. "My binoculars are in the trunk with the picnic food. You may borrow them if you like."

"Wow! Thanks!" Jonah said. His father was very particular about his binoculars.

"Jonah forgets things," Juliet said to Mr. Twist.

"Yes, he does," Mr. Twist said. "Except when he doesn't. So it's okay, you see."

"Oh," Juliet said. Then in a minute she said it again. "Oh."

Jonah leaned back in his seat and smiled. Even though his father sometimes didn't make sense,

Jonah thought he understood him. What he understood was that, to his dad, he was okay.

And there was someone else who was okay. Jonah sat forward suddenly in his seat, remembering.

"Dad!" he said. "We found Mr. Rosetti."

"Terrific," Mr. Twist said. "Where was he?"

"*Is*," Jonah said. "He's still there."

"Okay, where is he then?"

"In the hospital," Jonah said. "He's been there the whole time!"

He told his father about the letters from Portland and the long-distance phone call. Then he told him about his mother's call to the police.

"The police said we should try the hospitals first," Jonah said. "So we did. And there he was —right at Community Hospital."

"That's where my mother works," Juliet piped up. "She's the dietitian."

"What's wrong with Mr. Rosetti?" Mr. Twist asked. "Did they say?"

"No," Jonah said. "All they said is he's in fair condition. They said they couldn't tell us anything else unless we're next of kin."

"That's usually the rule," Mr. Twist said. "Still, it would be nice to know."

"Yeah," Jonah agreed. "But at least we know

he's okay. If he weren't, he'd be at the cemetery."

"Or in a UFO," Granville said.

"Not that," Jonah said. "They're fake."

"Prove it," Granville said. "Anyway, Mr. Rosetti would probably be having a lot more fun if he were in a UFO. Just think! He could be visiting Jupiter!"

"My mother could find out," Juliet said.

"Find out if he's visiting Jupiter?" Granville asked.

"No," Juliet said. "Find out what's wrong with Mr. Rosetti. Since she works at the hospital, I could ask her to find out."

"Hey, great!" Jonah said.

"Radical," Granville said.

Juliet went on, "But I need to know his whole name. In case there's more than one Mr. Rosetti."

"It's Vincent," Jonah said. "I know that from collecting his mail. But there's only one Mr. Rosetti, Juliet. He's special."

"Vincent Rosetti," Juliet repeated, like she was memorizing it.

Mr. Twist reached over and patted Juliet on top of her rain hat. "Good girl," he said. Then he said, "You guys are lucky to have a good friend like Juliet with important connections."

Jonah hesitated. Was he lucky? And was Juliet a friend? He wasn't sure. But he was really glad that Juliet was going to help find out about Mr. Rosetti. "Thank you, Juliet," he said.

"Yeah," Granville said, "thanks, ol' Juliet, ol' pal."

Juliet turned in her seat and beamed at Jonah and Granville. "No sweat," she said.

Jonah and Granville looked at each other and laughed. Jonah felt certain they were the only kids in the whole third grade to ever hear Juliet Fisher say "no sweat."

"I could even find out what he eats," Juliet said, "since my mother is the dietitian and all."

Jonah thought this over. "Okay," he said. "But if you have to choose, just find out what's wrong with him."

Mr. Twist turned onto Highway 1 at Half Moon Bay and headed south along the coast. Sunlight bounced off the Pacific Ocean to their right, and Jonah took several deep breaths of salt air. He felt good.

It wasn't the thought of seeing ugly elephant seals that made Jonah feel good, he was sure of that. So maybe it was because of Mr. Rosetti. In his mind, he heard himself say again, "Thank you, Juliet."

It was weird . . . as soon as he heard those

words in his mind, he felt even better. Maybe it had to do with public relations. Someday he would ask his father.

Some forty minutes later, Mr. Twist eased the blue Toyota into a parking space in front of a sign. The sign said Point Año Nuevo State Reserve.

Jonah, Granville, Juliet, and Mr. Twist trooped into an old barn that had souvenirs and a ticket-taker. Then they trooped out again and hiked along a trail to a clearing. Here, several people milled about waiting for the tour to begin.

Mr. Twist pointed to a man in a broad-brimmed hat and an orange vest. A badge on the vest said "Docent."

"That's your tour guide," Mr. Twist said. "Just stick with him and you can't go wrong. We'll eat lunch as soon as you return. There's a nice beach for a picnic at the other end of the parking lot. You'll find me in the car reading reports."

"If it rains, I'll eat in the car," Juliet said.

"If it rains," Mr. Twist said, "I'll eat my hat."

It was a long hike but an easy one over the bluffs. Every so often the docent stopped along the trail to point out a coyote bush or a place where Indians had once cooked supper.

"Where are the elephant seals?" Granville said to Jonah.

"I don't know," Jonah said. He was getting impatient, too. He had discovered that it was impossible to walk and look through binoculars at the same time.

Finally, the trail ran out. Ahead lay only sand dunes and thin patches of dune grass. Here and there red ropes were strung between poles.

"Stay on this side of the ropes," the docent said. "We don't like to disturb the seals."

Jonah didn't see any seals. All he saw were large sections of tree trunks scattered about on the sand.

"Logs," Jonah said.

"I'm never going to blend in with sand dunes and logs," Granville said. He sounded discouraged.

Juliet said she was getting hot. She opened her umbrella and used it to shade her face.

Suddenly, one of the logs raised its head. It looked around with big brown eyes. It opened its mouth and let out a long, drainpipe-like trumpet. Then it flopped back down on the sand.

"Holy moley," Jonah said. "And I thought it was a log!"

"Awesome," Granville said.

"Remember," the docent said, "state law forbids us to get any nearer than twenty feet. Anyway, it's safer—many of these seals weigh over three thousand pounds. You don't want to be in the way when one decides to move."

As the docent led them farther out on the dunes, there were more and more log-seals. Most seemed to be sleeping, but occasionally one lifted its head or rolled over.

Finally, when they cleared a rise, they could see elephant seals scattered over the dunes all the way to the horizon. And on a beach below, seals were clustered by the hundreds. Bull seals lifted their heads and trumpeted. Others used their flippers to throw great arcs of sand into the air and onto their backs. Some female seals were nursing babies, and one even gave birth as everyone looked on.

Jonah used his father's binoculars to watch as arriving seals lumbered in from the sea. He looked across the water at Año Nuevo Island where seals covered every inch of land. Never had he imagined that seals could be so huge. Or that there would be so many. Thousands upon thousands of elephant seals.

"I love them!" he said.

"Me, too," Juliet said. "They're not really ugly at all. They're just homely."

"I want one," Granville said.

Jonah laughed. "They're too big," he said.

"Maybe," Granville said. "But I'd let it have my room, if one would fit."

When the docent signaled that it was time to go back, Jonah was reluctant. He lagged behind, waving good-bye to first one seal, then another.

"Good-bye," he called. "Good-bye. I'll come see you again some time."

Occasionally, a seal would lift its head to look at him, just as though it understood.

Granville and Juliet reached the trailhead first. They stood waiting as Jonah arrived. Juliet took her rain hat and fanned herself with it.

"The tour guide had to go on ahead to get another group," she said. "He says we should hurry."

Granville unsnapped his canteen from his belt. "Have some," he said to Juliet.

Juliet looked startled, then took the canteen. "Thanks!" she said.

"Boy," Jonah said. "I'm sure glad we chose elephant seals for our report."

"Me, too," Juliet said. She handed the canteen back to Granville. "You know, I thought you chose them just to make me mad. But now I see why you like them so much. I'm sorry I complained."

Granville choked on a mouthful of water.

Jonah had to pound him on the back.

"I think it's time to go," Granville said.

"That's what I think, too," Jonah said.

The hike back seemed easier than the hike out. All three were in happy spirits. Once in a while Granville walked backward and wobbled his knees. This time even Juliet laughed.

When they got to a fork in the path, they stopped short.

"I don't remember this," Jonah said.

"Me neither," Juliet said.

"It wasn't here before," said Granville.

"But it must have been," Juliet said. "We just didn't see it."

"Or else we forgot," said Jonah. He knew all about forgetting.

Juliet looked one way and then another. Then she turned in a complete circle. "Are we lost?" she asked.

"Not yet," Jonah said.

"Question is," Granville said, "which way do we go?" He took off his helmet and scratched his head. "Hmmm," he said. Then he pointed to the right-hand path. "This way!" He popped his helmet back on and marched down the trail.

Juliet shrugged and followed.

Jonah shrugged and brought up the rear.

After a time it seemed to Jonah that the path was too winding. Then it seemed too narrow. Then it seemed too steep.

"Hey," he called. "I think this is the wrong way."

Juliet stopped. "Me, too," she said.

Granville stopped. "Could be a shortcut," he said.

"I don't think so," Jonah said. "It looks like it's going down to the ocean."

"Let me borrow your binoculars," Granville said. He looked through them for a long time. Then he scrambled a little way down the path and looked through them again. Then he came back up.

"You're right," he said. "It goes down to a beach. But at the other end of the beach are some steps. And the steps lead to a parking lot. I might have seen a blue Toyota in the lot."

"Then it's a shortcut?" Jonah asked.

"In a way," Granville said. "It's just not short."

Juliet looked doubtful. "Are you sure we're not lost?" she asked.

"Naw," Granville said.

"Maybe you should use your walkie-talkie," Juliet said. "Call for help."

"The only person I could call on this is my

mother," Granville said, "because the other end is in our kitchen at home."

"So call your mother!" Juliet said.

"What?!" Granville looked horrified. "Call my *mother*? Even if I wanted to, I couldn't, Juliet. It's way too far!"

"So why'd you bring it if you can't use it?" Juliet asked.

"What do you *think*?" Granville said. "For looks!" He thrust the binoculars back at Jonah. "Come on," he said, "we're wasting time here. Girls! Jeez!"

They continued hiking down the path. Juliet called out, "You'd better be right about this, Granville Jones!" She yelled this every few yards.

At the beach they stopped and passed around the binoculars. Sure enough, there was a parking lot up on the bluff at the other end. And there was Jonah's father's blue Toyota.

But there was something else. Halfway down the beach, about fifty yards away, lay a giant elephant seal.

"Wow!" Jonah said. "Our very own seal." He took off running down the beach.

"I'll race you," Granville said.

"Don't scare the seal," Juliet called after them.

For the first time in Jonah's memory, he won the race. Panting, he stopped and looked at the seal. Without a rope it was a little hard to tell how far away twenty feet was, so Jonah guessed. Then he added a few more feet to be safe.

He knelt down in the sand to look at the seal. Granville squatted beside him.

"Hello," Jonah said to the seal.

The seal rolled his liquid brown eyes at Jonah. Then he lifted his head and trumpeted.

"Don't worry," Jonah said, "we won't come any closer."

Juliet arrived out of breath. "Why is he here instead of with the others?" she asked.

"He's a spare," Granville said.

"Or maybe he's old and tired," said Jonah. He noticed that the seal had a leathery neck like the old alpha seals.

Just then the seal rolled slightly on one side. Then he rolled back again and flipped sand onto his back.

"Did you see that?" Juliet asked. "He has a name written on his back. It's Danny."

"Then he's an important seal," Granville said. "The scientists named some of the seals they're studying, remember."

Jonah picked up his binoculars again and

looked at the seal. He could see every detail from such close range. Then he saw a detail he hadn't expected. Something that shouldn't be there.

"Hey! He has fishing line tangled all around his head. And there's a hook. It's stuck by his eye!"

Quickly Juliet was on her feet. "We have to get help," she said. "That's very dangerous. He could go blind. And blind animals in nature die!"

"Oh, no," Jonah said.

"Granville, run! Find that barn and ask for a ranger," Juliet said.

"Why me?" Granville asked.

"Because I'm too hot in all this stupid rain stuff, that's why! And Jonah should go find his father so he won't worry. And," she added, with a trace of sarcasm in her voice, "because you're such a great pathfinder."

"Okay, okay," Granville said. "I'll go."

Juliet yanked the scarf from around her neck and handed it to Granville. "Wipe your face off first," she said. "Nobody will listen to you if you look too gooney."

Granville glared at Juliet. "You know, you're very bossy," he said.

Juliet glared back. "So?" she said.

"But, hey," Granville said with a shrug, "that's okay. I like bossy girls. Really I do. They're my favorite kind." He wiped his face and trotted off down the beach.

eight

WHEN JONAH woke up on Wednesday morning, the first thing he saw was his poster. It was propped up on his desk. And it was done. It had taken him ages to do it, to get all the details just right.

But it was worth it.

In the foreground was the giant bull elephant seal with the word Danny on his side. And off to the right were the ranger and the two scientists from the University of California field station. One of them held the medical kit.

Way in the background were four tiny figures. One was much taller than the rest. Another was dressed all in yellow. Another had a red top and blue pants. And one, the shortest, was very hard to see. He blended in with the bluff.

"Pretty good," Jonah said aloud.

He climbed out of bed and rolled the poster. He fastened it with three rubber bands. Then he got dressed for school.

"So today's the big day, huh?" his mother said in the kitchen.

"Yeah." Jonah opened a cupboard and pulled out a cereal bowl.

"Are you nervous?" his mother asked.

Jonah thought about this. Juliet had organized everything. She was going to give the parts of the report about range, reproduction, and diet. Granville was going to do size and natural history. He planned to act part of it out. And Jonah was going to do behavior observations because he had figured out some interesting things from watching the seals. He couldn't think of anything about all of this that should make him nervous.

"I guess not," he said at last.

"Good," Mrs. Twist said. "Glad to hear it. And here's something you'll be glad to hear: I think we can let Mrs. Einstein out of the bathroom now."

"Oh," Jonah said. He wanted to say something else. Something like "Hooray" or "Yippee." But it wouldn't come out. What stopped it was Woz. This meant that his mother had given up on Woz for good.

"I think Mrs. Einstein will be very glad to be out of that bathroom," she said. "Don't you?"

"I guess so," Jonah said. He stirred his cereal absently.

"Jonah, what's wrong?" his mother said. "I thought you would be delighted to have Mrs. Einstein running around the house again."

"Well . . ." Jonah said. "It's just . . . it's about Woz. And something else I was wondering about. I was wondering if we have any rats here."

"Rats? Well, I certainly hope not!" Mrs. Twist said.

Jonah hoped not, too. But that was just the thing—he didn't know for sure. There was the matter of some missing sunflower seeds.

Jonah had stashed little clusters of seeds in various places around the house. Out-of-the-way places where his mother wouldn't notice them. But some of the clusters had disappeared. The ones in the dining room and kitchen were gone. And, although Jonah had replaced the seeds once, they were gone again.

Jonah had looked carefully around these rooms for Woz. But no luck. Now he longed to ask his mother if she'd found the seeds and swept them up. But he couldn't do that. Asking if she had found the seeds would involve admitting that he had hidden them in the first place. This seemed like a bad idea.

Jonah's cereal had grown soggy. He gulped it down anyway and put his bowl in the sink.

"I have to go," he said. "I'll let Mrs. Einstein out after school when I can move her litter box."

His mother hugged him. "Have a good day," she said, "and good luck on your report."

"Thanks," Jonah said. He gathered his rolled poster, his lunch box and binder, and jogged toward Granville's house. He didn't want to be late. Juliet had said to be on time or she'd kill them both. Jonah didn't believe that. But he did believe she'd be mad, which was almost worse.

Granville was waiting on his front steps. He was dressed in brown pants and a tan shirt. He was holding a baseball bat, and on his head was a fur hat.

"Cool hat," Jonah said.

"It's coonskin," Granville said. "See the tail?" He shook his head. "It used to belong to my dad. It's kind of smelly, but it's just for today so I don't mind." He handed the hat to Jonah.

Jonah sniffed it. "Phew!" he said. He handed it back. "What's the bat for?"

"A club, of course," Granville said. "See, I'm the white hunter, and I walk up to the elephant seal and—*bonk*!—I hit him over the head. Then the seal dies and—*presto*!—I have thousands of pounds of seal blubber. What do you think?"

"Mean." Jonah shuddered.

"Yeah," Granville said, "and easy. Too easy.

That's how I'm going to show that the elephant seals almost became extinct. They never had a chance."

Jonah thought about the seal named Danny. He imagined someone dressed like Granville, but three times as big, bonking it on the head. It gave him a lump in his throat.

Juliet was already in the classroom when Jonah and Granville arrived. She was standing at her desk, pulling papers out of her binder.

"I thought you were going to be absent," she said. She was wearing a blue skirt with a matching jacket and a white bowtie blouse. She reminded Jonah of a TV newscaster.

"We have to have everything ready," she said, "in case we're called on first."

They weren't called on first. Robbie, Greg, and Kevin were called first. They gave a report on moles. They had an elaborate map of mole hills and tunnels. There were marks on the map showing where they had dug to find the mole. Robbie said his father was upset about the holes in their backyard.

Juliet spent the morning arranging and rearranging some papers on her desk. Her notes. She didn't seem to be listening to anyone.

At morning recess, Jonah and Granville played

nation ball with the class. Juliet didn't play. She
didn't watch, either. She stood on the sidelines
and walked up and down. Sometimes she wrung
her hands.

When the bell rang, Granville said, "I hope
we're called to give our report soon. Juliet looks
like she might be getting sick."

Jonah looked at Juliet. She was as white as her
blouse. "I think you're right," he said.

"Besides," Granville said, "this cap really
stinks."

At long last Mrs. Lacey called their group.
"Granville, Juliet, and Jonah will give the next
report," she said.

The three of them stood in front of the chalkboard. Jonah was careful not to wiggle while
Juliet talked. Those were her orders—don't
move while other people talk.

Juliet told about all the fish the seals ate, and
how they didn't eat a thing during the months
they came ashore to have babies and mate. Some
kids giggled when she talked about the mating,
but Juliet ignored them. She would have made a
great newscaster.

Then Granville told about how big the elephant seals were. "The babies are big for Labra-
dor retrievers," he said, "and the grown-ups are

small for aircraft carriers." Then he acted out how the seals almost became extinct.

Finally, it was Jonah's turn. He told about how the seals moved like waves when they heaved themselves along the beach. And he told how they flipped sand on themselves.

"The scientists don't know exactly why they flip the sand on themselves," Jonah said. "Like maybe it helps keep them warm, or maybe it helps keep them cool.

"But I was watching the seals for a long time, and I think I figured out some other reasons. One is that it helps keep flies away. Another is that it feels good. I know this because when I sit on the beach and dribble sand on my legs, it feels really good."

Jonah showed the map that Juliet had made him draw. And he showed the poster he'd drawn because he wanted to. Granville told how they had helped the seal named Danny, and that the ranger and the scientists had thanked them.

"We might have even saved its life!" Juliet said.

At the end of the day, Mrs. Lacey told everyone how well they had done on their reports. "All of your reports were above average," she said. "I'm very proud of you."

She walked up and down the rows of seats

handing out slips of paper. Each paper had a space for the student's name, the subject, and the grade.

Jonah looked at his. Then he turned it quickly upside down on his desk. He waited a second, then picked up the corner to peek at it again.

"Hey!" Granville thumped Jonah on the back. "We got A's!"

"I know," Jonah said. "Or at least *now* I know. I thought it might be a mistake." He turned his paper back over and stared at the large red A. It was the first he had ever gotten.

Next to it, in Mrs. Lacey's curling script, was a word. It took a moment for Jonah to make it out. "Wonderful!" it said.

Jonah turned in his seat to look at Juliet. He expected to see her grinning, too. But she was busy tidying her binder as though nothing had happened.

When the bell rang, Juliet was ahead of Jonah and Granville as they filed out.

"Juliet, wait up," Jonah called. He caught up with her at the bottom of the steps. "Aren't you happy?" he asked.

"About what?" Juliet said.

"This!" Jonah said. He waved his slip of paper at her. "We got A's!"

"Oh, that," Juliet said. "I always get A's."

"I *usually* get A's," Granville said. "Sometimes I don't bother."

"Not me," Jonah said. "I *never* get them."

Juliet smiled a satisfied kind of smile. "You did when you worked with me," she said.

Jonah turned this over in his mind. "That's true," he said. "I'll work with you again if you want.

"And not just because of the A's, either. You're . . . well . . . you're not as bad as I thought, Juliet."

"Ha!" Juliet said. "And you're not as bad as you *were*." She turned to Granville. "You're the one who is really bad, Granville. You smell!"

"Hey," Granville said. "It's not me. It's the hat!" He took it off and threw it on the ground. Then he jumped on it. "Honest, it's the hat," he said.

Jonah and Juliet laughed.

As soon as Jonah got home, he went straight to the refrigerator. He took a magnet and fastened his slip of paper to the refrigerator door. This was where his mother posted all the important notices. And this, Jonah knew, was an important notice.

Jonah raced upstairs to the bathroom. Mrs. Einstein meowed a greeting as he went in.

"Guess what?" Jonah said. "You're free!"

Mrs. Einstein cocked her head first to one side, then the other. "Come on," he said. "Follow me."

Jonah picked up the litter box and carried it downstairs. He put it in the back hall, then returned for the food bowls.

Mrs. Einstein was still standing in the bathroom. Jonah thought she looked puzzled.

"Come on," he said again. "You're free. Sprung!"

This time Mrs. Einstein seemed to understand. She scampered after him down the stairs.

Jonah filled her bowls with fresh food and water. Then he watched as she ate.

"I got an A today," he told her.

Mrs. Einstein munched happily on her food.

"And something else," Jonah said. "Juliet found out what's wrong with Mr. Rosetti. He broke his hip. She says that's a really big deal if you're very old."

Mrs. Einstein continued munching. Jonah thought she was the perfect audience. She never interrupted.

"Juliet also says Mr. Rosetti eats a low-salt diet," he said. "Whatever that means."

Todd appeared in the kitchen doorway. His backpack was slung over one shoulder and his track shoes over the other.

"So!" he said. "I see the killer is on the loose again." He went to the refrigerator and got out a carton of milk.

"She's not a killer," Jonah said. "Besides, Mom said she could be out."

"Well, I suppose that makes sense," Todd said. He opened the milk and drank straight from the carton. "After all, there's nothing left for her to kill. That is, unless you're going to start buying her live mice like they do for snakes. Are you going to buy mice for her?"

"Very funny," Jonah said. "Anyhow, she would only play with a mouse. She'd never kill it."

"Says you," Todd said.

"I can prove it," Jonah said. He ran to the living room and turned up couch cushions until he found Mrs. Einstein's toy mouse.

"Look," he said, displaying the mouse to Todd, "no teeth marks. All she does is push it around and chase it."

Jonah dropped the mouse on the floor next to Mrs. Einstein. She sniffed it, looked at Jonah, then cuffed at the felt mouse. It skidded across the floor and underneath the refrigerator.

"Smart mouse," Todd said. "It knows a killer when it sees one."

Jonah groaned. "Now how am I going to get it out?" he asked.

"Don't ask me," Todd said. "I'm not into doing favors for killer cats." He dropped the empty milk carton in the trash and left the room.

Mrs. Einstein stretched out on her stomach in front of the refrigerator. She stuck a paw underneath and mewed in a tiny, crackling voice.

"Poor Mrs. Einstein," Jonah said. "First you get blamed for killing Woz, then you get locked up, and now you've lost your toy."

Jonah went into the back hall and rummaged for the yardstick and his mother's utility flashlight.

"Maybe I can get your mouse with these," he said when he returned.

Jonah flattened himself on the kitchen floor next to Mrs. Einstein. He shone the beam of the flashlight under the refrigerator.

"Yuck. It's really dirty under here," he said. "And the dust balls are the same color as your mouse."

He shoved the yardstick under the refrigerator. Then he dragged it forward in a sweeping motion. Wads of dust came out with the yardstick. But no mouse.

"Drat," Jonah said. He shone the light under the refrigerator again. If only he could see the . . .

He spotted something way in the back. A

lump. He couldn't be sure at first. Was it the mouse? He squirmed to get a better view.

It was bigger than a mouse. The flashlight caught the glow of two red eyes. If it wasn't a mouse . . . Jonah strained to see. Was it . . .? Could it be . . .? Tiny whiskers quivered in the dust.

"*Woz!*" Jonah shouted. "It's Woz! And he's alive!"

nine

"Mom, you're going to make me late," Jonah said on Sunday morning.

Mrs. Twist stood at the kitchen sink slicking Jonah's hair down with a wet comb. "I'm still not sure it's wise to sneak into a hospital," she said, "but at least you'll look respectable if you're caught."

"Don't worry," Jonah said. "I told you, Juliet's mother will help us. And she told Juliet nobody will really mind as long as we behave. Granville promised he won't even wobble his knees."

"Well, that's something at least." Mrs. Twist laughed. She set down the comb. "All ready?" she asked.

"Almost," Jonah said. He took his slip of paper off the refrigerator. "I might want to show this to Mr. Rosetti," he said. He folded it carefully and put it in his pocket.

"Okay," his mother said, "but be sure you bring it back. I enjoy looking at it."

"I will," Jonah said. Then he added, "I might get another someday."

"That's fine with me, Jonah. I wouldn't mind looking at more than one."

Jonah thought about this. "If I get too many, we might run out of room," he said.

"Not to worry," his mother said. "If you get that many, I'll get another refrigerator."

Jonah laughed. "That's fair," he said.

Granville was just coming up the front walk as Jonah left the house.

"I thought you might have forgotten," he said.

"I might have," Jonah said. "But I didn't."

Granville was holding a brightly wrapped box in his hands. He held it up for Jonah's inspection. "What do you think?" he asked.

"You did it!" Jonah said. "It's great." He studied it more closely. "It's birthday wrapping," he said.

"Yeah, well, it was the best I had," Granville said. "But I don't think Mr. Rosetti will mind, do you?"

"I don't think so," Jonah said. "Mr. Rosetti doesn't mind much."

"Except his sister," Granville said.

"Right," Jonah said. "Except his sister."

It was a long walk down Manzanita Avenue

and Sierra Boulevard to Community Hospital. But they reached the hospital lobby with ten minutes to spare.

Finally, a large-boned woman in a starchy white uniform approached them. A white net covered her hair.

"You must be Jonah Twist and Granville Jones," she said. "Juliet has spoken so much about you, I think I'd know you anywhere."

"Ulp," Granville said.

"Thanks for helping us see Mr. Rosetti," Jonah said.

"I'm glad to do it, Jonah," Mrs. Fisher said. "Actually, I did some checking, and it seems Mr. Rosetti hasn't had any visitors since he's been here. So I don't mind bending the rules a bit for a good cause.

"I do expect *you* to be very careful to obey the hospital rules, however," she went on. "Such as speaking quietly . . ."

"And no running, and no touching equipment," Jonah said. "We know. Juliet told us everything. Three times."

"Juliet's very bossy," Granville said.

"I know," Mrs. Fisher said brightly. "I think she'll make a splendid doctor, don't you?"

She led Jonah and Granville down one long

corridor and then another. Then she led them into an elevator marked "Service." She pushed the button for the sixth floor.

As they stepped off the elevator, Mrs. Fisher held her finger to her lips. "Very quiet, now," she said. "It's just down here. Room 604. I'll come back for you in a while."

Jonah knew a way to walk which would make his shoes squeak loudly. And he knew a way to walk so they wouldn't squeak at all. He chose the quiet way. Granville walked behind, knees straight and the box held carefully in his hands.

Jonah read the name tag on the door to room 604. "Vincent Rosetti," it said. He put his hand on the doorplate and pushed.

Mr. Rosetti's thick white hair showed over the top of the magazine he was reading.

"Hi, Mr. Rosetti," Jonah said.

Mr. Rosetti lowered the magazine. He looked at Jonah and blinked. Then he blinked again. Then a large smile broke across his face.

"Why, Jonah Twist!" he said. "You're about the last person I expected to see here. And about the most welcome, too." He stretched out his hand.

Jonah grabbed it and gave it his best shake. "I missed you," he said.

"And I missed you," Mr. Rosetti said. "And Granville! What a wonderful surprise!"

110

Then a look of doubt crossed Mr. Rosetti's face. "Wait a minute," he said. "How did you get in here? I wouldn't want you boys to land in any trouble on my account."

"We won't," Jonah said.

"It's an inside job," Granville said. "We had help."

"From Juliet Fisher," Jonah explained. "And her mother."

"And who is Juliet Fisher?" Mr. Rosetti asked.

"She's a . . ." Jonah hesitated. Well, he may as well say it, since it was true. "She's our friend," he said. "Her mother is the dietitian here."

"And Juliet is the bossiest person in the world," Granville said. "But it's okay once you get used to her."

"She can't be more bossy than my sister," Mr. Rosetti said. "Violet is a champion bosser."

That reminded Jonah of something. "She's coming tomorrow," he said. "She told that to my mother."

Mr. Rosetti scowled. "I know," he said. "She called to let me know she'll be staying for a while. To 'help out' as she puts it. Of course, one of the ways she wants to help out is to put me in an old people's home. And now that I've broken this hip, she thinks she has the perfect excuse."

"Is your hip better?" Jonah asked.

"Where's your cast?" Granville asked.

"My hip is much better, thank you," Mr. Rosetti said. "And soon it will be good as new. Better than new, actually, because they've given me a replacement. That's why I don't have a cast: I had an operation instead."

"Wow," Jonah said. "Like when the muffler on your car wears out they just give you a new one?"

"Very much like that," Mr. Rosetti said. Then his soft brown eyes shone fiercely. "And if my sister thinks she's going to put me in an old people's home, she's got another think coming. I'm neither too old, too infirm, nor too addled to live alone!"

Granville grinned. He nudged Jonah in the side. "Now?" he asked.

"Now," Jonah said.

"We brought you some help," Granville said. He reached across the rails of Mr. Rosetti's bed and put the box on his lap.

The box jiggled back and forth.

"We know it's not really your birthday," Granville said. "But that's the only wrapping I had where the air holes wouldn't show."

"Air holes!" Mr. Rosetti said. "Don't tell me . . ." He pulled the ribbon off the box and lifted the lid.

112

"A kitten!" he said.

The black-and-white kitten looked at Mr. Rosetti. Then it hopped out of the box and settled, purring and kneading its paws, on Mr. Rosetti's stomach.

"Well, I'll be!" he said. He stroked the kitten's head with his big, freckled hand. "This must be one of your kittens, Granville. But how can a kitten be a help?"

"It was really Jonah's idea," Granville said. "So the kitten is from both of us."

Jonah felt uneasy. He couldn't really tell if Mr. Rosetti wanted the kitten.

"It's so you won't have to go to an old people's home," Jonah said. "See, your sister says you're too old to live alone. So the next time she says that, you say, 'But I don't live alone. I have a kitten!' Get it?"

"I'm beginning to," Mr. Rosetti said. Then he chuckled. "It'll stump her, all right." He chuckled some more. "In fact, it's exactly the kind of reasoning that will make her madder than a wet hen!" He chuckled even harder. "She might . . . she might just pack up and go home early! Ho! Ho! Ho!"

Jonah laughed, too. He laughed because Mr. Rosetti was laughing. And because Mr. Rosetti liked his plan. And he laughed because the kitten was riding up and down on Mr. Rosetti's stomach.

Mr. Rosetti wiped his eyes. "Well," he said, "now I am papa to a kitten. I wonder what I should name her."

"Him," Granville said. "It's a him."

"I named mine Mrs. Einstein," Jonah said. "It was in case she turned out to be smart. And she did, too. Even Todd is starting to like her now that she helped find Woz. Of course, she might have helped lose Woz in the first place. But Todd has a padlock on Woz's cage now, so it's okay." He took a deep breath. He didn't know if this was making any sense to Mr. Rosetti.

"Anyway," Jonah went on, "I was bringing Mrs. Einstein to meet you. That's how I found out you were missing."

"I thought you went in a UFO," Granville said.

Mr. Rosetti laughed. "No such luck," he said.

The kitten had fallen asleep on Mr. Rosetti's stomach. He tickled it gently on the cheek until it opened its eyes.

"I don't know how I'm going to keep him in the hospital, though," Mr. Rosetti said. "I believe the hospital has even more rules against pets than they do against visiting children."

"That's okay," Granville said. "We'll take care

of him until you get home. In fact, that's part of the present. We'll take care of him any time you're away."

Mr. Rosetti winked at Granville. "Even if I go away in a UFO?" he asked.

"Well . . . if you go in a UFO, *Jonah* will take care of the kitten," Granville said. "Because *I* want to go with you!"

When Mrs. Fisher stuck her head in the door and said it was time to go, Granville put the kitten back in the box. Jonah held it while Granville tied the ribbon snugly in place.

"Jonah," Mr. Rosetti said, "I'd like to ask you a favor."

"Sure!" Jonah said.

"I wonder if you'd stop by my house," Mr. Rosetti asked. "You see, when I fell and broke my hip, I wasn't able to do much more than dial 911. I'm afraid I left some of my tools lying out in the backyard. They've been on my mind a good deal."

"No sweat," Jonah said. "They're in your garage. I already put them there."

Mr. Rosetti sighed and leaned back against his pillows. "Jonah Twist," he said, "you are a very good and thoughtful friend."

"Thanks," Jonah said with a grin. "That was really the plan."